"Do you know how to drive a car?"

Hunter smiled. Not like the carefree young man who had won Hope's heart, but still, it had the power to catapult her back to one of the most painful times in her life.

"I do—or at least I think I do. I can operate a tractor. The idea is basically the same." He glanced past her to *Daed* and Naomi. "We have to act fast for Conrad." The concern he had for his friend was there on his face. He'd fight for Conrad with everything inside him. He just hadn't cared enough for her to keep fighting for them. The realization hurt.

"I'll check in the car. Maybe they left their phones there along with the keys."

Hope forced the heartbreak aside. "I'll keep watch over these two with *Daed*. Hurry, Hunter," she added, because she couldn't get the man's words out of her head.

You're all dead, you hear me? Dead. He won't think twice about killing all of you. If that were true, then every second they wasted was one they might need to stay alive.

Mary Alford was inspired to become a writer after reading romantic suspense greats Victoria Holt and Phyllis A. Whitney. Soon, creating characters and throwing them into dangerous situations that tested their faith came naturally for Mary. In 2012 Mary entered the speed dating contest hosted by Love Inspired Suspense and later received "the call." Writing for Love Inspired Suspense has been a dream come true for Mary.

Books by Mary Alford

Love Inspired Suspense

Forgotten Past
Rocky Mountain Pursuit
Deadly Memories
Framed for Murder
Standoff at Midnight Mountain
Grave Peril
Amish Country Kidnapping
Amish Country Murder
Covert Amish Christmas
Shielding the Amish Witness
Dangerous Amish Showdown
Snowbound Amish Survival

Visit the Author Profile page at LoveInspired.com.

SNOWBOUND AMISH SURVIVAL

MARY ALFORD

LOVE INSPIRED SUSPENSE
INSPIRATIONAL ROMANCE

LOVE INSPIRED SUSPENSE
INSPIRATIONAL ROMANCE

ISBN-13: 978-1-335-72289-8

Snowbound Amish Survival

Recycling programs for this product may not exist in your area.

This edition published by arrangement with Harlequin Books S.A.

For questions and comments about the quality of this book, please contact us at CustomerService@Harlequin.com.

Love Inspired
22 Adelaide St. West, 41st Floor
Toronto, Ontario M5H 4E3, Canada
www.LoveInspired.com

Printed in U.S.A.

My soul waiteth for the Lord
more than they that watch for the morning:
I say, more than they that watch for the morning.
—*Psalm* 130:6

To my husband, Monte. Heroes aren't defined by words. They are forged through the hard moments of everyday life. That's you, my love. You are my true hero.

ONE

Outside, the wind howled around the corner of the house with enough fury to shake windows. The blizzard had continued to grow in strength with nightfall. It sounded like a wild animal raging.

"It's getting worse by the minute." Midwife Hope Christner did her best to pull her focus from the distraction. Her expectant mother patient and *gut* friend, Naomi Hartzler, was nervous enough without the added stress of the storm. Naomi needed her full attention. *Gott* would take care of the weather.

"Try to relax. I'm almost done." Hope patted her friend's arm. Naomi had been on edge since her pregnancy began—and with *gut* reason. This was Naomi's fourth pregnancy. The first three had ended in miscarriages.

Hope finished her exam and came to the same conclusion she'd had when she'd arrived at the home. "I'm afraid it's another false alarm," she said as gently as possible. The second one in as many days.

A flood of tears filled Naomi's eyes. Hope sat beside her and put her arm around Naomi's shoulders. "I'm sorry. This isn't what you want to hear, I know."

Naomi wiped her eyes. "*Nay*, it's not. I'm so worried, Hope. Every moment that passes without the *boppli* coming, I can't help but feel as if something bad will happen to our sweet little bundle." Her voice broke into a sob as she touched her swollen midsection.

Hope's heart ached over the previous losses Naomi and Conrad had suffered. "I know it's hard, but everything is well with the *boppli*. It will be different this time, I genuinely believe that."

Naomi visibly gathered her composure and squared her shoulders. "I want to believe you, and I know it's a few days early, but I'm ready for my *dochder* to make an appearance. Now. I really want to hold her in my arms and reassure myself she is *oke*." She heaved out a weary sigh and swung her legs over the side of the bed. "Conrad, too. We do not wish to bury another baby." Fresh tears fell from Naomi's devastated face.

"And you won't," Hope stressed and prayed it was true. "*Gott*'s timing is perfect. When it's right, the *boppli* will come, and you and Conrad will be wishing for more sleep." Her attempt to lighten the moment fell short. "*Komm* into the kitchen. I'll make you some tea to settle your nerves." Hope helped Naomi to her feet. With her hand ensconced in her friend's, she stepped from the bedroom and almost collided with Conrad, who waited patiently for news. No doubt praying for a different result this time.

"Another false alarm," Naomi told him in a weepy voice.

"But all is well with the *boppli*?" Conrad looked Hope's way, and she nodded.

Conrad smiled. "We'll have our child soon enough, *fraa*, you'll see."

Naomi perked up at her husband's reassurances. "You're right. It will happen before we know it."

"That's my girl." Conrad kissed his wife's cheek.

Together, they walked down the hall to the kitchen.

Conrad glanced out the window. "The snow is coming down harder, I could barely see the road enough to get you, Hope. You should stay here tonight. Abe will understand."

When Conrad had arrived at the home Hope shared with her father to tell her Naomi believed she was in labor, the snow had already been falling for hours.

"That is a *gut* idea. *Denki*, Conrad."

"You are *willkumm*." Conrad headed to the living room. The sound of the door to the wood-stove being opened was followed by logs being tossed on the fire. This storm had all the makings of one of the worst in many years.

Hope pumped water into the kettle. Outside, fat snowflakes swirled around in the light projected from the lantern. Even with the stoves in the kitchen and living room, the chill had begun to permeate through the house. Hope held her hands near the flame beneath the kettle to warm them.

"The last time I saw so much snow was back when we were but *kinner*," Naomi murmured as she looked through the chilly glass. "You remember that winter? You and me and Hunter went sledding at the hill near here, and we all got caught in that snowstorm." Naomi turned with a smile that soon evaporated. "I'm sorry."

Hope did her best not to show how much it still hurt to think about what might have been. "No, it's *oke*." Yet even after more than five years since the ending of her relationship with him, it wasn't easy to think about, much less talk about, Hunter.

The teakettle whistled. Hope started and

swung toward the sound, a nervous laugh escaping. She'd been on edge since Conrad had showed up at her door, and she had no idea why. Just a bad feeling that wouldn't go away.

"Is anything wrong?" Naomi asked, her watchful eyes on Hope's face.

Letting go of the bad feeling wasn't easy. Hope reminded herself she was a strong woman who had delivered babies under some of the most inconvenient circumstances. She wasn't one to jump at shadows.

"Just the storm, I suppose. It's got me on edge." She retrieved three cups and some tea from the cupboard. Plopping teabags into the mugs, she poured in hot water.

"Here you go." Hope turned toward Naomi with the cup in her hand. Before Naomi had time to accept it, an explosive crash came from the living room, followed by a loud thud. Cold air rushed through the house. Her bad feeling doubled.

The teacup rattled in Hope's hand. She bit back a scream and managed to place it on the counter without dropping the cup.

She was about to ask Conrad what had happened when an angry voice Hope didn't recognize yelled, "Where's the midwife? I know she's here."

A stranger had broken into Conrad and Naomi's home, looking for her. She couldn't even begin to understand it.

Hope captured Naomi's frightened eyes and shook her head. *Don't say a word*, she mouthed. She couldn't think of a scenario where what was happening didn't end badly.

"She's not here." The distress in Conrad's voice was unmistakable. He spoke louder than normal as a warning to Hope and Naomi to stay hidden.

What sounded like a scuffle taking place had Naomi grabbing for Hope's arm. Fear crackled the air between them. Both were terrified for Conrad's safety.

Hope searched the kitchen for something to use as a weapon. She grabbed one of the knives in a block and started for the living room. Conrad was in danger. He needed help.

"You're lying," the same man growled. "I know she's here because her old man told us."

Her footsteps faltered. Her father. This man threatening Conrad had gone to her home and forced her *daed* to tell him Hope's location. All sorts of terrible thoughts flew through Hope's mind. *Daed* was not well, hadn't been since the first stroke happened several years back. Since then, he'd suffered a series of milder ones.

"Stop lying and tell us the truth," the angry

man continued. "Or do I have to use this to make you talk?"

Us. There was more than one man. Hope wouldn't be able to fight them by herself even with the knife. She had to think about Naomi and the *boppli*'s safety.

"Put the gun away." Conrad's response sent a chill down Hope's spine. The men were armed. "I told you the midwife isn't here. It's just me."

"Just you? Where is your wife? She's pregnant—the old man told us so. Doesn't make sense she'd leave the house in this weather." It was only a matter of time before the men searched the house and found her and Naomi.

"My wife went to see her *mamm*—her mother." Conrad stuttered over the explanation. He was being so brave. "There's only me."

"I don't believe you." Sounds of another, more intense, struggle ended with the unmistakable crack of a gunshot. The noise resounded through the small house, followed by Conrad's blood-curdling scream. It sent chills through Hope's body. Her friend was hurt. How bad?

Not another word came from Conrad. Naomi started past Hope to aid her husband, but Hope caught her arm. "You can't go in there," she whispered.

Naomi made the whimpering sound of a woman terrified for her *mann*.

The noise didn't go unnoticed. "What was that? I thought you said you were alone," the same man demanded. Her friend must still be alive for now.

"You two, go check it out. Bring her to me. Now."

Hope pulled Naomi along with her to the back door.

"I can't leave Conrad," Naomi moaned and struggled to free herself. Hope didn't let her go. As she forced the door open, the wind snatched it from her hand and slammed it against the wall. Everyone inside would have heard the noise. There wasn't much time.

Hope grabbed the two coats hanging near the back door and ushered Naomi out into the cold. She worked with trembling fingers to help her friend into the coat and slip the second one on. Surviving meant getting out of sight quickly.

The two fought their way across the yard while driving snow and ice struck like needles against their faces. It was impossible to see much beyond the distance of their hands in front of them. The whiteout conditions soon swallowed them up, and Hope could no longer spot the house through the storm.

"I don't see anyone," a man's voice said. "They could be anywhere."

"Doesn't matter." Another person spoke. "You heard the boss. They can't get away."

Hope kept her hand on Naomi's arm and hurried her along. "You must think of the baby," she urged after Naomi cast a fearful look behind them. She couldn't imagine how hard it was for her friend to leave her husband behind. "This is what Conrad would want. If they catch us, we won't be able to get him help." She gathered Naomi close in an effort to protect her from the biting wind.

As a child, Hope had made this place her playground. At one time, the house where Naomi and Conrad lived had belonged to her family—until the property dispute between Hope's father and his dear friend Levi Shetler had destroyed so much.

Her *daed* believed Levi had deliberately crossed the boundary line between her family's and the Shetlers' and had logged the woods that contained many young trees. Levi had denied it, but the proof was there in the downed trees, and the Shetler family had been logging near the property line around the same time.

Daed had been heartbroken that his friend would betray him in such a way and then deny it to his face.

After her father had suffered a series of

strokes, he'd sold the house to Conrad and moved himself and Hope to a smaller farm.

"What if they kill my Conrad?" The words tore from Naomi's throat.

"They don't want Conrad. It's me they're after." Still, would they risk leaving witnesses behind? They'd shot Conrad to make him talk. These men were ruthless. What could they possibly want with her?

Naomi's steps slowed.

"You are doing great. Don't stop," Hope told her while trying to sound positive. "We must keep going. This weather is not *gut* for you or the baby." When they reached the treed area between properties, the woods offered some relief from the elements. Hope hurriedly buttoned Naomi's coat and then hers for more warmth.

Snow from previous storms had piled up in drifts close to two feet in depth in places. Trudging across it drained Hope's energy at a rapid rate. She couldn't imagine the struggle Naomi was going through with the extra burden of the child.

"Don't look back. Just keep walking," she warned when Naomi glanced over her shoulder. Hope was terrified of what might be coming up behind them.

Neither she nor Naomi was dressed for the outdoors, even with the coats. Hypothermia was a great risk, and Hope couldn't bear the thought of Naomi carrying her *boppli* this far to lose it to the elements.

"How much farther?" The wind whipped Naomi's words all around, and Hope almost didn't catch them.

"Not much." She did her best to shield Naomi from the cold and tried to keep it together. Each step required all the energy she possessed to complete. Giving up would be so easy. She turned her face away from her friend and brushed crystalized ice tears away.

A sound behind them had Hope tugging Naomi into the protection of a patch of trees. They crouched low while her heart went wild.

Naomi leaned heavily against Hope. The temperature and the freezing snow and ice was putting her at risk every moment they were out in the elements like this.

Hope drew in a breath and leaned a little away from the tree. No one. What had she heard?

It didn't matter. Their lives were in danger from more than those men chasing them.

Please, Gott, *keep us safe.*

She stepped from behind the tree along with Naomi. Nothing was visible in her limited view.

Keep going. Don't stop.

Just as her strength was all but gone, the trees began to thin in front of them. They were almost out of the woods. Beyond the woods lay Hunter Shetler's place.

Every time she heard his name—said it—thought it, even—her heart broke over the past and the love they'd once shared.

Going to Hunter for help was something Hope could not have imagined until now. But she and Naomi were all out of options. There was no other choice. She'd do whatever necessary to save her friend. Even if it meant reaching out to the man who'd broken her heart.

Something banged against the front of the house loud enough to wake Hunter Shetler from a troubled sleep.

He forced out a breath, while his sleep-filled eyes darted around the room lit only by the fire glow and a lantern that was ready to burn out.

Had the sound been part of his dreams, like the gunshot he'd thought he'd heard earlier?

Another series of knocks—coming from the door—confirmed this wasn't a dream. Someone was outside. A second later, a familiar female voice jumped out to him from the past, chased by the same hurt he experienced every time he thought about her.

"Hunter, it's Hope. Please, open the door. We're in danger."

Danger? Hunter shot to his feet. His fuzzy

brain tried to make sense of it. Hope was the last person he ever expected to be standing on his porch at any time, much less in the middle of the worst storm of the season. And she'd told him she was in danger. All sorts of disturbing reasons popped into his head.

He crossed the room in two quick strides and yanked the door open. A snow-covered Hope stood before him, teeth chattering. Her terror-filled hazel eyes clung to his. Huddled beside her was his neighbor, Naomi Hartzler.

"Was iss letz?" he asked, his attention going to Naomi's swollen middle. Had something happened to the baby? Where was Conrad?

Hope glanced nervously behind them, as if expecting someone to appear. Hunter's fear level doubled. "Please, can we come in?"

He stepped back. They must both be frozen as snow continued to blow inside the house. *"Jah,* sorry."

She ushered Naomi across the threshold and immediately shut the door. She slid both the lock and dead bolt into place. The action did nothing to clear up his concerns. "Hope, what's going on?"

In almost five years, they hadn't spoken a single word to each other. The accusations leveled at his *daed* by Abe Christner still had the power to make Hunter's blood boil. Even worse than the anger was the betrayal he'd felt by Hope. It still cut through to his heart. She'd believed her father over him.

A few days after the argument, Hunter's *daed* had seen a battered truck out near Abe's woods. A couple of *Englischer* men were coming from them carrying chain saws. When they'd spotted *Daed*, they'd quickly left the area and his father hadn't seen them again. He'd found several cut trees and believed the men had been illegally harvesting timber around the community.

Daed had told Abe about the discovery, but Abe refused to believe his friend.

"I didn't know where else to go," she said. Her eyes frantically searched around the living space that at one time was to be his and Hope's home. "I was so afraid they'd catch us."

"Who are you talking about?" he asked because he didn't understand anything about what she'd said so far.

"The back door." Her eyes flashed fear his way. Without answering his question, Hope ran to the rear of the house and flipped the locks into place.

By now, Hunter had become genuinely worried. He swung to the nearby window and glanced out. Nothing but a deluge of snow swirling around out there. Yet Hope would not be here now if everything were *oke*. What kind of trouble was heading their way?

Hope reached her friend's side and led Naomi to the chair Hunter had recently vacated. "Sit and warm yourself. You need to stay off your feet as much as possible after what happened."

She grabbed the quilt Hunter's *mamm* had made for what would have been their wedding present, and snugged it around Naomi's trembling body. Hope came over to where he stood, her pretty face marred with the weight of what she and Naomi had just been through.

"Some men broke into Naomi and Conrad's home. They are armed and they shot Conrad." As she explained, Hope lowered her voice and looked back at Naomi, who stared into space, silent tears falling. "The man in charge sent others after us. We managed to make it here without being spotted, but I don't know where they are, or how badly Conrad is hurt." Her troubled gaze held his. "Hunter, they came to the house looking for me," she stressed.

Nothing about what she said made sense. Conrad was hurt? Armed men had broken into the home and shot his friend. Hunter's hands fisted. Anger rose inside. His first instinct was to charge over to the house and…and what?

His jaw tightened. He loved Conrad like one

of his *bruders* and would do anything to save him. No matter the cost.

"Who would wish to harm you? Why would they shoot Conrad?"

She lifted her palms and shrugged. "I have no idea. As I said, they were looking for me, and it clearly has something to do with me being a midwife."

"I don't understand." How could Hope assisting babies into the world warrant armed men coming after her?

Hope went to Naomi and felt her hands before nodding. "*Gut*, you are warming up."

Naomi turned her tearful face to Hope. "I am so worried."

Hope squeezed her shoulder. "Your husband is strong and resourceful. You mustn't lose faith. *Gott* will protect him."

Hunter's thoughts tangled over themselves. His friend was hurt. Conrad had been so excited about the new life growing inside Naomi. With each passing month, he'd allowed himself to believe this time would be different and Naomi would carry the child full term. After everything they'd been through, now this?

Gott, I don't understand Your ways sometimes.

While he watched Hope with Naomi, Hunter tried to keep thoughts from going back to the argument that had ultimately torn them apart. Still today, he couldn't accept she'd refused to even listen to him. That she would believe Hunter's *daed* or his *bruders* capable of doing such a thing. She'd told him she loved him and yet she'd broken his heart. For years, Hunter had struggled to let go of the resentment he felt. Seeing her now proved he hadn't been able to accomplish it yet.

Hope turned and found him watching her. He tore his glance away as she returned to his side. Somehow, he must get past the anger and resentment if he was going to be of any use to his friends. And to Hope.

"Why do you think this is connected to what you do?" A simple calling like being a midwife would have nothing to do with such acts of violence, surely.

She searched his face before answering. "Because the one man specifically asked for the midwife. Hunter, he said he'd been to my home. They forced my father to tell them where I'd gone. If they hurt him…"

He couldn't begin to imagine what it must have taken to get that information from her *daed*. It troubled him that armed men were singling out Hope because of her job.

"Has something unusual happened recently in your work? Is someone following you, perhaps? There has to be a reason why they'd be looking for you specifically."

Hope shook her head. "No, there's nothing," she insisted. "I've had several deliveries around the community recently, but all went well, and there were no problems during or after the births. In fact, I checked on the mothers and babies recently." She blew out a breath. "There's been no one unusual hanging out around the house, either. I don't understand why they are coming after me, but I'm afraid, Hunter. I'm very afraid."

She lived a simple life with her *daed*. Beyond being the midwife for the area, Hope sold quilts and wall hangings at one of the shops in the community. So what did such innocent behavior have in common with men willing to use violence to get what they wanted?

For the most part, the community consisted of peaceful people who honored *Gott* with their lives, and yet this wasn't the first time violence had leached its way into the West Kootenai community in the form of outsiders. There had been other incidences that had become personal, involving members of his family. It had proved to Hunter bad things happened no matter where you lived.

Hope glanced back at her friend. "I was so certain they would spot us before we reached your place." She told him how she and Naomi managed to escape the house and about their frantic trek through the woods separating the two properties. She ran a visibly shaking hand over her eyes. "With the weather, they hopefully weren't able to see which direction we went. The falling snow should cover our footprints." She suddenly clutched his arm. "But they have Conrad, and he could be seriously hurt. We have to do something."

Conrad needed him. He wouldn't let his friend die. No matter what had happened between him and Hope, or how broken he'd felt when she'd chosen to end things, this was Conrad. His friend. He'd protect Naomi and Hope because that was what Conrad would wish.

"*Komm* lock the door behind me. You and Naomi stay here where it's warm." Hunter reached for his shotgun. "I'm going after Conrad."

Hope grabbed his arm before he'd taken a single step. "You can't. They'll kill you. We have to get help."

He looked at the face of the woman he'd once loved and tried not to think about the life they'd planned together. The dreams.

"I'll be *oke*." Still, she didn't let him go. "Perhaps they gave up and left. Conrad could be bleeding out. I have to go."

He slowly loosened her fingers and noticed her soaked dress and wet prayer *kapp*. She was shaking from the cold and probably also from shock over what had happened.

"You're shivering." Hunter leaned the shotgun against the door and grabbed an extra quilt from the chest where he kept them. He wrapped it around her shoulders.

That little wrinkle between her brows was one he recognized right away. In the past, Hope had had a habit of looking at him like she was right now whenever he'd done something she hadn't understood. His protective gesture must have confused her.

He'd grown up with her—knew what she felt simply by the expression on her face. It reflected when she was angry with him. Or teasing. He'd loved all those things about her and had told her he was going to marry her since they were kids. She'd laughed at him until soon after they'd finished their *Rumspringa* and he'd asked her to be his wife for real.

Yet when the first test to their commitment had come, they hadn't survived it. Perhaps it had been *Gott*'s way of opening both their eyes to the truth. They were not meant to be together.

Hunter's jaw tightened. It still hurt, and he'd struggled to let go of the pain, to give it entirely to *Gott* like his *mamm* had pleaded with him to do since the breakup. So far, it hadn't worked. His and Hope's past had been written and could not be changed. He had this moment—now—to make the right choice. And he would do whatever possible to save his friend's life.

He grabbed the shotgun again. "Take care of Naomi." Anger crept into his tone. Hunter struggled to soften his next words. "I will be careful. I'll ride the mare over and walk in before I reach the house and can be spotted."

He picked up a box of shotgun shells because he was almost certain he'd need the added protection. Hunter started for the door.

The thought of facing off with armed men in the middle of such a storm was not a *willkumm* one, yet he had to do something. He and Conrad had grown up together. Since Conrad and Naomi had moved next door, they helped each other out with the planting and harvesting. Hunter had stood with his friend and watched him mourn each lost *boppli*. Rejoiced with him at the prospect of Naomi carrying this child to full term.

Taking his coat from the peg beside the door, Hunter shoved his arms into it before slipping on his warm boots. "Be sure to lock the door behind me," he reminded Hope before lighting another lantern to take with him. He disengaged the dead bolt and reached for the doorknob. A sound outside—barely distinguishable above the wind—stopped him from opening it.

While Hope's frown deepened, Hunter quickly reengaged the dead bolt and listened. The wind wailed its mournful sound. But it was another noise that captured his attention.

A board squeaked. He recognized it because he'd been meaning to replace the loose one on the steps. Every single time he stepped up on it, that same squeak reminded him of the needed repair. Now, he wondered if it might be the one thing to save all their lives.

"Oh, no," Hope whispered next to him. She'd heard it, too. "They tracked us here."

He clasped her arm and put distance between them and the door.

Naomi gathered the quilt around her body, her fearful eyes watching the door as if expecting those men to barrel inside at any moment.

Hunter cocked his head and listened carefully.

Only one squeak. She'd said there were more than one man following them. Where were the others?

Hunter slipped his arm around Hope's shoulders and glanced to Naomi, who huddled beneath the blanket, her frightened eyes glued to the door. Above the noise of the weather, someone moved around on the porch. The hairs on the back of Hunter's neck stood at attention. He placed a finger over his lips. If they didn't make a sound, perhaps the men would leave.

How had they found the two women through the storm? Disjointed thoughts flew through his head. None made sense.

Snow-muffled footsteps traversed the porch. A flashlight swept across the front of the house, visible through the curtains. After what felt like forever, the light disappeared. Hunter released the breath he'd held. A heartbeat later the front door splintered open. Snow flew in its wake, covering everything nearby. A man dressed entirely in dark clothing filled the entrance.

Hunter let Hope go. "Run. Get Naomi and leave out the back."

He pushed her toward Naomi and aimed the shotgun at the man. "That's far enough. You have no right to be here."

Out of the corner of his eye, he noticed Hope standing perfectly still in the middle of the room. Why wasn't she moving?

"Hope, get out of here," he urged, but she didn't budge.

"I can't." She pointed toward the back and he realized another person had entered the house.

The first man stepped inside and shut the door. Hunter never lowered the weapon. "I said, that's far enough."

The man wasn't looking at him but at something beyond Hunter's line of sight.

Hunter spun around in time to see the second man grab Hope's arm. Before he could react, something hard struck the side of his head. Excruciating pain was followed by the world around him spinning out of control. Hope. She was the last thought in his mind before blackness encroached through the spinning world. His eyelids slammed shut. Hunter fought it, but it was a losing battle. He stumbled. His feet deserted him. He hit the floor hard. The ground and the darkness swallowed him up.

TWO

"Hunter!" Hope screamed in horror as Hunter dropped to the floor unconscious. The man in black had struck the stock of his weapon against Hunter's head, effectively ending the threat he posed.

The other man tightened his hold on her when she tried to free herself and go to Hunter's aide. His fingers dug painfully into her arm the harder she pulled.

"Let me go. He's hurt." She continued to struggle to no avail.

Her captor lowered his head until he was inches away from her. Dark eyes held an anger that seemed to radiate from him. "You're not going anywhere but with us."

With us. They planned to take her. Panic swept through her body. What about Hunter and Naomi? Conrad?

"Get on your feet." The man who had struck

Hunter towered over Naomi, waving the gun in her face.

Naomi shrank deeper into the chair. "I said, on your feet." The gunman grabbed her arm and forced her up.

"Leave her alone. She's pregnant." Hope dug at her restrainer's fingers, but it was useless. He was much stronger than she was.

Naomi moaned and clutched her midsection while her panicked eyes sought out Hope.

"It's okay. He won't hurt you." She tried to reassure Naomi of something she had no idea was true.

"You think we won't hurt her or you? You're wrong. Let's go." The man near Naomi aimed his weapon at Hope. "I said, let's go."

"What about him?" Hope's captor indicated Hunter.

"I'll take care of him." The words sent chills through Hope. "You get these two back to the house." He shoved Naomi toward Hope.

The man holding Hope tried to drag her toward the door, but she dug in her heels.

"I am not going anywhere without Hunter."

Forcing Naomi along with him, the leader was in Hope's face in two strides. "You're not calling the shots here, lady. Now, start talking. Where's the young woman you helped to deliver her baby? Where's Penny Jenkins?"

Shock rippled through Hope's body. What did Penny have to do with these men? "Why are you looking for her?"

He obviously didn't like being challenged. "I'm asking the questions. Where is she? You'll take us to her if you want to live."

The threat sent chills down Hope's spine. She did her best to keep her voice steady. "I don't know where Penny is now. She told me she was just passing through the area when she went into labor."

Though lying wasn't something Hope condoned, when it came to saving a life, she would do whatever necessary to protect her friends and Penny.

Penny's small cabin on the other side of the mountains was remote and sat some distance from the closest road. Hope had thought it odd Penny would choose such an isolated place to live alone. When she'd asked Penny about the baby's father, she'd been told the relationship hadn't worked out. Now, Hope wondered if perhaps Penny might be running from someone. Was the man who tried to force Hope to go with him Penny's husband?

The man calling the shots let Naomi go and snatched Hope from his partner's grasp. He jerked her to within a few inches of his anger-distorted face. "You're lying. She's here somewhere. We know she inherited her grandmother's house somewhere near your Amish community. She has no place else to go. Where. Is. She?" Each word was delivered with seething rage.

Penny's grandmother had lived here before? Hope had no idea. She remembered the older *Englischer* couple who had once lived in Penny's house. The husband had passed away a few years earlier.

Somehow, Hope kept from showing her fear and stood up to the man. "I am not lying." She flinched when he shoved the gun against her head, and her heart threatened to explode.

"Perhaps she will get you to talk." He looked at Naomi. "You want me to shoot her like I did her husband?"

The words threatened to take Hope's legs out from under her. He would do harm to a pregnant woman?

He smiled an ugly smile and seized Naomi's arm again.

"No, please." Naomi tried to back away.

He held the gun against her belly. "You want your friend to lose her baby because you refused to talk?"

"Let her be!" Hope yelled, her anger overtaking the horror. "It's going to be *oke*." She held

Naomi's frightened eyes and tried to make it be so.

He didn't lower his weapon. "Tell me where Penny is, and you and your friend can go back to doing whatever you were doing before we arrived."

Out of the corner of her eye, she saw Hunter's hand move slightly. He was regaining consciousness.

Hope forced her attention away before one of her assailants noticed. "I don't know anything about her grandmother, but Penny isn't here in the community any longer. She told me she only stopped because she went into labor." A quick look confirmed Hunter's eyes were open. His fingers stretched out toward the shotgun. She had to keep these two distracted.

The man calling the shots looked at her through narrowed eyes. "I don't believe you. Where's this house she inherited from her grandmother?"

Hope swallowed several times to quench her dry mouth. "I have no idea. Like I said, she came to my house to deliver the baby and, when she could, she left. Penny told me she and the baby were going to see relatives in Colorado." None of it was true. The story that spilled out was as much a surprise as how easily it came.

"Enough games. This lady and her baby are

dead if you don't start telling me the truth," he yelled, with the gun still pointed at Naomi.

Hope believed he wouldn't think twice about killing Naomi and the child. Her friend's life depended on what she said next. She looked him in the eye without flinching. "I am telling you the truth. Penny left and she told me she was going to visit family in Colorado. Maybe you don't know everything about her life."

The man's face burned with anger. For a second, Hope believed he would strike her.

Hunter now had the weapon in his hand. The minute he made his move, those men would be gunning for him. She had to keep stalling to give him time to get it in the firing position.

"Penny said her family lived near Denver." Hope took a chance and named the only city in Colorado she could remember.

Without blinking, the man shoved Naomi at his partner and started dragging Hope to the door.

She jerked her head at Hunter in time to see him leap to his feet. A second later, her captor noticed. He released Hope and whipped toward Hunter. Hope grabbed Naomi from the second man's clutches. They ducked behind the sofa and out of sight of the battle to come.

"Drop your gun," Hunter said with dead seriousness. Hope inched far enough back that she could see Hunter. He kept the shotgun aimed at the leader. The man reacted quickly and opened fire. Hunter hit the floor, and the bullet meant for him lodged in the wall near where he'd stood moments earlier.

As the second man grabbed for his weapon, Hunter fired. The man dropped to the floor and grabbed his side. "I'm hit," he wailed. "I'm hurt bad."

Hope tugged Naomi lower behind the sofa as a war filled the room.

Please keep Hunter safe, she prayed with all her heart. She'd brought this trouble to his door. This was her fault. Would it end up costing Hunter everything?

He'd never shot another man before, but Hunter had done so now without hesitation and with a steady hand because, if he didn't stand and defend, others would die.

The injured man writhed on the floor. His partner fired off several rounds. Hunter dived for the cover of the sofa as one shot came close enough to graze his arm. When silence returned, Hunter peeked out in time to see the shooter grab his partner by his collar and drag him behind the wall leading to the bedroom.

Hope stumbled to her feet and pulled Naomi up and alongside her until they reached Hunter.

His coat sleeve flapped open where the bullet had ripped through it and his shirt. Blood stained both garments.

"You're hurt." Hope's troubled eyes found his.

"It is nothing." He dismissed the injury to his arm and felt around his head to spot where he'd been struck. His fingers connected and he winced.

Out of the corner of his eye, Hunter noticed the barrel of a weapon peeking from behind the wall where the men hid.

"Watch out." Hunter pushed the women down low before backing the men up with another round of shots. "We have to get out of here," he said once the two were out of sight again.

He gathered Hope and Naomi close and crossed to the door quickly. Slinging the shotgun strap over his shoulder, he stepped outside with the women. "If we can make it to the barn, we'll have something between us and them." Huddled against the weather, they started down the steps.

Just getting across the yard proved its own battle. Snow mixed with sleet made it seem as if they were walking through a wall of needles. Hunter was relieved when the barn came into his line of sight.

He urged everyone around to the side while glancing behind them. The dim light from the house backdropped the two men as they left the porch and headed for the barn. Hunter ducked out of sight before their flashlights could pick him up.

"They're coming," he whispered. If they hid inside the barn and those men found them, they'd be trapped. Their only option was to get to Hope's place, which was the next house down from his, though still some distance away. "If we can reach your place, we can check on your *daed* and then take the buggy to the phone shanty to call for assistance."

At the back of the structure, the woods had begun to encroach on his property. Hunter checked behind them first before they entered the trees. After they'd covered some ground, he looked over his shoulder. So far, there was no sign of the men coming up behind them. They were probably checking inside the barn.

All he could think about was Conrad. Hope didn't know how serious Conrad's injuries might be, but Hunter had witnessed firsthand how dangerous these men were. There could be others out here looking for them. Or worse, waiting at Hope's house for them to walk into a trap.

"Our only chance to help Conrad is to reach the phone shanty and call the sheriff." On foot, it would be impossible.

Naomi stopped and grabbed her stomach,

doubling over. Hope rushed to her side. "Is it the baby?"

Naomi pulled in several breaths and shook her head. "I don't think so. Just a cramp." Yet her worried eyes held Hope's.

"You are doing great. Stay strong. For Conrad and the *boppli*."

Naomi managed a couple of shaky breaths before nodding.

As they continued walking, Hunter found himself wondering about something he'd overheard the one man say. "They were questioning you about a woman called Penny. Why do they want her?" Hunter didn't recognize the woman's name.

"I have no idea." Hope shrugged. "Penny is a sweet young *Englischer* who showed up at my house and asked for my assistance. She told me Sadie Zook from the bakery gave her my name and how to find me. Penny delivered a healthy baby boy a few days ago at her home." Hope cast a watchful eye to Naomi before continuing. "I checked on her yesterday. She appeared fine. Nothing seemed to be bothering her. I don't understand why this is happening."

That made the situation all the more troubling. What reason could they possibly have to come after a *mamm* with weapons?

"I told them Penny had the baby at my house

because the last thing I wanted was for them to find out where she lived. She's a new mother raising a child on her own."

Still, there had to be a reason those men were looking for her. Hunter found the idea of such threatening men coming into the community disturbing. "Where is the child's *daed*?"

Hope looked at him. "She didn't really say other than he was no longer around."

Was it possible this Penny was running from her husband? "Whoever these men were, she's in danger. They are determined."

Hunter stopped suddenly. Just the faintest of noises above the storm had alerted him to something nearby. He listened for a handful of seconds. Nothing. Still, after what had happened, they had to be careful.

"Someone's coming. Hurry, let's get out of sight." He looked around for a safe place to hide. A cluster of lodgepole pines created a natural refuge among the other trees growing in the woods. "Over there. Quickly." He assisted Naomi into the pines.

They scarcely managed to get out of sight before tromping sounds came from nearby. Hope grabbed Hunter's arm while her frightened eyes glued to his. He gathered both women close in a protective gesture as two flashlight beams came to within a few inches from where they hid. With the light, those men would be able to see their recent footsteps. The thought cleared from his head when one of the men spoke.

"They've been here. I see three sets of footprints. We're on the right track. Let's keep going."

Labored breathing sounded far too close to their hiding place. "I don't care if we're right on top of them. I can't go on. I'm losing a lot of blood. We have to turn back."

The first man's irritation exploded. "Are you kidding? They'll go to the police. I don't want to go back to jail."

Jail. At least one of them had committed a crime before.

"Well, I can't go on any longer." The man's voice was barely audible over his heavy breaths.

An annoyed-sounding sigh followed. "Go back by yourself. I'll keep on their footprints. Best not to leave any witnesses behind. They've seen our faces. They can identify us, and I, for one, don't want to cross him. You saw what he did to his cousin."

Those chilling words clenched Hunter's stomach.

"I can't make it by myself." Each word sounded forced from the speaker. "You're gonna have to help me. I'm about to pass out."

A string of curse words followed. "Fine, but

for the record, I don't like it and I'm going to tell him as much. And if this comes back on us, I'm not going to jail, I'll promise you that. I'll make sure of it."

The other man grunted. "Come on. Give me a hand, will you? Chances are with the one woman pregnant, it will slow them down. They'll freeze to death out here before they reach another home."

Even after the pair's movements grew faint, Hunter didn't trust it wasn't a trap. "Let's stay out of sight a little while longer," he whispered while going over every single word the men had said. They were obviously working for someone they both feared.

He poked his head around the tree. No one stood close, waiting to pounce. "I think they've gone. We'd better keep moving in case there are others out here looking for us."

Walking through the deep accumulation slowed their progress tremendously.

It felt like they'd been walking for hours when Naomi said, "Can we stop for a second? I need to catch my breath."

Naomi obviously struggled with exhaustion. Her strenuous breathing grabbed Hunter's attention. When she clutched her side again, he became worried.

The stress would not be *gut* for the child.

He led Naomi over to a downed tree log and brushed off snow. "Rest." She nodded and held her side while gasping for air.

"I'm really worried about her," Hunter said when he returned to where Hope kept watch on the path they'd traversed.

"Me, too. She can't lose this child." She bit her bottom lip as she studied Naomi's huddled form.

"How are you holding up?" From where he stood, her fear had almost become a living thing.

"I'm so worried." She turned her troubled face up to him. "About Conrad. Penny. Naomi. My *daed*. If they hurt him…" Her voice broke off.

Hunter struggled to find something comforting to say and fell short.

Hope and her father were close. Had been most of her life. Since her *mamm* died tragically after battling a severe case of the flu a few months before Hunter and Hope became engaged, her relationship with Abe had grown ever more important.

Rhoda had been the family rock and the only one who could keep Abe's stubbornness under control. Hope tried, but she was his *dochder*, and Abe was not fond of listening to anyone. Rhoda's death had just about broken Abe. He became filled with bitterness. Hunter often wondered if that bitterness had played a part in the feud between their fathers.

"We don't know what happened to Abe for sure. They could have used intimidation to force him to talk. As soon as Naomi has a chance to catch her breath, we'll keep going."

Hope glanced past his shoulder to where Naomi sat. The wind caught strands of her loosened raven black hair and tossed it in her face. Her prayer *kapp* was soaked, along with her clothing. There really hadn't been time for her or Naomi to warm up before the attack at his house.

He skimmed her troubled face and still couldn't believe she was standing here with him again. It felt surreal.

In the last five years, he and Hope had had virtually no contact—not even at the biweekly church service. He'd done his best to avoid both her and Abe, yet most days, he was forced to drive by the piece of property where Abe accused his *daed* of illegally logging. He still remembered the day he and his *bruders* had gone to walk the property line marked by some stacked stones put there years ago by his *daed* and Abe. The half dozen downed trees were evidence someone had been logging the property recently, but it hadn't been them.

Hunter's *daed* had tried to tell Abe this but as usual, he'd refused to listen. Hunter had tried to speak with Hope about it. She'd vehemently defended her father. With he and Hope on opposite sides, there'd been no way of fixing things between them and so she'd called off the wedding.

His jaw tightened. Would this bitterness be in his heart forever? "We should get going. Naomi needs to be out of this weather." He turned away too quickly. Winced. The knot on his head was a reminder of what bad men were capable of doing. His head hurt like all get-out, which wasn't doing much for his stomach.

Hope didn't miss his reaction. "How bad is it?" she asked gently.

"It's nothing." He dismissed her concern with a shortness she didn't deserve. Hunter collected himself. "I'm really sorry this is happening to you," he said to make amends. "To Naomi and Conrad. Your father." Sorry that violence had once again worked its way into their community. Into many innocent lives.

"And to you. You didn't deserve any of this, either." Her hazel eyes held his. She sincerely meant what she said, and his chest tightened. Holding on to his anger with her had made the breakup almost bearable. It humbled him that she could be so generous when he didn't deserve it.

Hunter cleared his throat. "The sooner we reach your *haus*, the better. I don't trust that one man not to come back."

She visibly shivered. "I don't want to even think about another run-in with those dreadful men."

He stayed at Hope's side as they returned to Naomi.

"How are you feeling?" Hope asked her friend.

Weariness had carved itself on Naomi's face. "I'm *oke*. Just worried about my Conrad."

Hunter shared the same fears for his friend. He lifted Naomi to her feet. "We will do everything we can to get help for Conrad."

Keeping Naomi close between them, he and Hope started walking again. The woods held the brunt of the wind at bay, and yet Hunter could feel himself slowing down from the cold. Just putting one foot in front of the other had become a challenge.

When he wasn't sure he could continue, the woods thinned and the property clearing near Hope's home came into view. Those men had been here before and he was worried they'd returned, but there was no other option.

"Denki, Gott," Hope whispered through chattering teeth.

As they stepped from the woods into the clearing, goose bumps traveled up his arms. The dark house did little to ease Hunter's concerns. What if those men had circled back while they'd been in the woods? Everyone here could be walking straight into an ambush that none of them were equipped to survive.

THREE

Often, Hope struggled to think of this place as home despite the years she'd lived here. Yet it had never appeared more welcoming than it did now. She ran toward it as fast as her exhausted limbs would allow. All she could think about was finding her ailing *daed*.

"Hope, no." Hunter's warning reached her ears, but she didn't slow down. Her father could be in trouble.

Reaching the house, Hope rushed up the steps. The delicate curtains her *mamm* had sewed were one of the many things that reminded her of what she'd lost. The drapes were open. She caught a glimpse of the dark living room beyond. No sign of her *daed*.

Her heart pounded against her chest as she reached for the door handle. Hunter stepped up behind her and covered her hand with his. "Let me go in first," he whispered. The shotgun, no longer slung across his shoulder, was gripped in his free hand. "We don't know if they left men inside."

She hadn't considered the possibility there might be armed men in her home. The idea of them holding her father hostage terrified her.

Hope stepped away. Yet all she could think about was rushing inside to find her father and assure herself those men hadn't hurt him.

Hunter slowly turned the knob, then moved across the threshold with Hope and Naomi inches behind.

The quiet of the house stretched out without a peep. If there had been people here, they were now gone.

"*Daed*. Are you *oke*?" Hope called out when she could no longer stand not knowing. The only answer was silence. She turned to Hunter. "Where could he be?"

"I'll check the rest of the house. If he's here, we'll find him. Stay with Naomi. Let me check."

The fire in the stove had faded to a few glowing embers. Proof that her father hadn't been in the living room in quite some time. When she'd left with Conrad to check on Naomi, it had been dark for a while.

Hope guided Naomi to the sofa near the stove and placed the quilt she kept there over her friend's shivering body. All the while, she listened for any sound from her *daed*.

She quickly stoked the embers, then added several logs. "I'm going to help Hunter," she told Naomi because she was worried about her father. "Stay here, where it's warm, and rest." Naomi barely acknowledged her words.

Hunter was preparing to open her *daed*'s door when she reached him. He glanced her way before slowly turning the handle. Pushing the door open, he stepped inside with her close behind.

The moment she saw her father's broken body lying on the floor near his bed, her hand flew to her mouth. "Oh, *Daed*."

Why wasn't he moving?

Hope ran to her father and dropped to her knees. He'd been badly beaten, his face swollen and bloody. "*Daed*. Oh, *Daed*." She shook him gently.

Abe groaned low and slowly opened his eyes. When he saw his daughter, his pained expression eased. "You're safe. I've been so afraid." He struggled to sit, but grabbed his side.

"No, *Daed*, don't try to move. You're hurt." She gently felt around for broken bones.

Abe pushed her hands away and scooted to a sitting position against the bed. "I'm fine. Are they gone?"

"*Jah*," she assured him. "What happened?"

"Several men attacked me in my bed." Abe glanced past Hope to where Hunter stood, and his mouth immediately thinned. "Why is he here?" Hope shifted Hunter's way. She would always remember the rift that tore them apart. The downed trees that had been glaring proof of someone trespassing on the property and logging the family's trees. And the only people who had access to the place were her father and the Shetler family. Still, Hunter had stepped up and done his best to protect her and Naomi. "He saved us. Me and Naomi. If it wasn't for Hunter, we might both be dead." She explained about the attack that came quickly and Conrad being shot.

"It must be the same people," Abe muttered without looking at Hunter again. "I had no idea they were even in the house until they barged into my room and demanded to know where you had gone."

That they could do such harm to a feeble man made her sick to her stomach. "They are looking for Penny, *Daed*. That's why they want me. To help them locate her." She told him about the two men questioning her about Penny. "Let's get you off the cold floor." She put her arm around her father's waist but didn't have the strength to lift him by herself.

With an exasperated sigh, she turned to Hunter. "Can you get him to his feet?"

Hunter didn't hesitate. Hope moved aside and

watched Hunter lift her father effortlessly off the floor.

As soon as *Daed* became steady, he pushed Hunter away. "I can make it on my own. I don't need *your* help. It's just a few bruises."

Hunter held up his hands.

"At least let me clean your cuts." Hope lit the lantern near her father's bed and stayed close to him as he lumbered toward the kitchen.

Naomi rose as they entered the room. She clamped her hand over her mouth at the state of *Daed*'s injuries.

"You should be resting," Hope reminded her. "As soon as I tend to my father, I'll get you something to wear so you can change out of those wet things."

Naomi didn't answer. Her wide eyes followed their progression into the kitchen.

Her father lowered his weary body to the chair he normally sat in at the head of the table.

Hope pumped water quickly and grabbed a washcloth along with some antiseptic to treat the wounds.

While she carefully cleaned her father's cuts, her anger rose at the bloody marks left behind by those men's fists. They'd beat a sickly old man to try to get information out of him. What would they do to Conrad? He didn't know anything about Penny—certainly not where she lived. He would be useless to them and he could identify them.

Penny had asked Hope not to mention anything about her delivery, indicating only Hope and Sadie knew. The woman had worn loose clothes, sunglasses and a thick knit cap when outside. Most probably wouldn't even realize Penny had been carrying a child. At the time, Hope hadn't thought much of it. Now she wondered if perhaps Penny had been trying to disguise her appearance to keep herself hidden from an abusive husband.

"How does that feel?" she asked her father once she'd finished.

Abe patted her hand and staggered to his feet. *"Gut. Denki, dochder."* Holding his side as if he'd bruised some ribs, he trudged into the living room and lifted the poker to stoke the fire.

Her father had a stubborn streak that went way beyond being self-reliant. It had been there for as long as Hope could remember. After *Mamm* passed, the stubbornness was joined by bitterness and anger.

Hope bit back the request on the tip of her tongue for him to go to the hospital. It would be a waste of breath.

She put the supplies away and went to her room to change into dry clothes. Hope grabbed one of her dresses for Naomi, along with a fresh prayer *kapp*, apron and warm stockings. Though the dress would be snug with the baby, at least it wouldn't be wet. Slipping into her father's room, she found a change of clothing for Hunter. With the items in her arms, she returned to the living room.

She handed the dress to Naomi and helped her to her feet. "You can use my room to change. Let me take your coat. I'll hang it near the fire to dry."

Naomi moved like someone in a daze.

Hope hung both their coats near the wood-stove and turned to Hunter, who stood near the window, watching the front of the house. Though Hunter and her father would always be on opposite sides of the two families' feud, he hadn't done anything deserving of her father's anger now, and he had brought her and Naomi safely here.

Hope stopped beside him and studied his profile. She felt the need to apologize for *Daed*'s behavior.

His thick black hair was plastered against his head, covering the wound. The slight bump at the bridge of his nose was a reminder of a baseball game and the fly ball Hunter had missed.

"Let me take your coat to dry it." She helped him slip out of the coat. "I'm sorry about what my *daed* said earlier."

Hunter turned those piercing blue eyes her way. There was a sorrow reflected there that seemed to have become part of his being. "You father feels the way he feels. We both understand why."

Even sadder because it was true.

"I have something dry for you to put on. You can change in my father's room." She handed him the clothes.

"Denki." He accepted the items and stepped away to change. Hunter was taller than her father. The clothes would not be a *gut* fit, but at least he would be dry.

She arranged his coat near hers and Naomi's.

Once he'd changed, Hunter returned to the window where she stood watching the storm continue to batter their world. "It's not letting up."

"We aren't safe here. Eventually, they'll return." Hunter voiced her same concerns. "Is Naomi *oke* to travel? The trip through the woods was hard on her."

Naomi sat hunched over on the sofa, the quilt wrapped across her shoulders. *Daed* had claimed the spot beside her. Neither spoke a word.

"She's strong and the *boppli* appears healthy. I believe she will be able to make the trip."

The only *gut* thing to come from the conditions was that the snow had probably covered their footprints by now. If the uninjured man decided to continue his trek to silence them, he'd have a hard time finding their tracks.

"*Denki*, Hunter. With everything that happened, I haven't properly thanked you for coming to our aid. I am grateful."

He stared down at her with an unreadable expression before answering. "It was the right thing to do. I would have done the same for anyone."

He hadn't done it for her. His answer struck like a blow. But what had she expected? He still blamed her for taking her father's side when he'd made the accusations. But how could she not? Hope was all her *daed* had, and she would always have his back.

Hunter cleared his throat. "I'll get the buggy harnessed. As soon as it's ready, we should leave."

She turned from the swirling whiteness outside. "It will be warmer using the enclosed buggy." Yet Hope worried about their older mare. "Poor Penelope isn't accustomed to such weather and she's old." Penelope had belonged to the family for years.

Hunter's expression softened. "She's a *gut* mare. Penelope will do fine." He grabbed his coat and slipped it on, then removed one of the lanterns from near the entrance. Hunter lit it before taking up the shotgun he'd leaned against the doorframe.

"Wait." He swung back to her. "I'm coming with you." His brows shot up. "The work will go faster with two," she said before he could voice his concerns. "And Penelope knows me. She'll be more inclined to agree to going out in this weather."

Without waiting for his response, Hope put on her warmest coat and shoved her feet into her rain boots. She stepped out into the freezing weather along with Hunter. Guiding the horse and buggy through such a dangerous storm wouldn't be easy, but they had no choice.

As she and Hunter left the porch, he glanced up at the sky. "I was hoping this would have blown itself out by now." The unease in his tone was unmistakable.

They fought their way across the yard to the barn. Hunter struggled against the wind to get the door open while Hope kept a close watch behind them. With the snow, it was impossible to hear anything. Those men could be right on top of them and she and Hunter wouldn't know it.

A tremor chased through her limbs. If they ran into those men again, she had a feeling it would end in deadly consequences.

* * *

Hunter led the old mare over to the buggy. As he and Hope worked to get Penelope secured, he was reminded of the many times they'd performed this same task together.

He'd known he loved her since they were *kinner*. Hunter had come to Hope's defense after she'd fallen and skinned her knee when Kemp Verkler, the *shool* bully, had pushed her down. They'd been inseparable from then on.

Hunter turned away and snugged the straps near the mare's head. Regret weighed heavy on his heart. Being with Hope again was a reminder of how badly things had ended for them.

He would never forget the angry scene between his *daed* and Abe. Abe's insistence that the Shetler boys had logged his property against his wishes, taking down many of the young trees he'd planted to replace ones previously harvested. The piece of property was years away from being ready to log and everyone in the Shetler family knew this. Hunter couldn't believe Abe would think his father or *bruders* would do such a thing.

It seemed unimaginable that the argument would destroy a childhood friendship, much less his and Hope's future.

But it had been too much to move beyond for

both of them. Hope had come to him in tears and told him it was over.

"I'll get the door," he said over his shoulder. "Hop inside where it's dry."

A moment passed before she climbed into the buggy.

He moved to the doors and threw them open. Hunter waited as she pulled the buggy outside. Once he'd secured the barn, he climbed in beside her and urged Penelope toward the porch. He and everyone in the house was running out of time.

Hunter hopped to the ground and held out his hand. When she took it, that same special feeling he'd had in the past whenever Hope held his hand was just another hard reminder that even though they were not the same people, some things never went away.

"I'll assist Naomi," Hunter said. "You should probably be the one to take care of Abe." He opened the door and stepped inside along with Hope and a flurry of swirling snow.

Abe was slumped back on the sofa watching the fire. Naomi sat beside him, her troubled gaze filled with questions. After so many miscarriages, the last thing Hunter wanted for her was to lose this precious *kinna* she carried.

"There's no sign of those men," he assured Naomi. "But we must hurry. I'll help you out to the buggy." Hunter assisted her into the coat she'd worn before.

Abe stubbornly refused Hope's help. He grabbed his jacket and struggled to get his arms through. "Where are we going? In this storm, we can't go wandering recklessly about." He addressed the angry question to Hunter.

Hunter explained the need to reach the phone shanty before those men found them. He guided Naomi out the door and into the buggy while Hope trailed close behind her father.

Once the two were safely in the back, Hunter returned to the house and gathered extra blankets for warmth before hurrying back outside to the buggy.

He shook the reins and Penelope started away from the house. Visibility was barely to the horse's muzzle. Tension strung tight between his shoulder blades as he leaned forward. "It's hard to see anything." He was worried. About them. The mare. These conditions weren't *gut* for man nor beast. He looked to Hope. "We have to make it to the phone. Otherwise, there will be no one coming to save Conrad or us."

Fear dawned quickly on her face. "How are those men getting around in the weather?"

"They probably have a four-wheel-drive vehicle or something like that. Maybe they are using snow chains."

Somehow, Hunter managed to keep the buggy on the tree-lined drive though he hadn't once been to this house.

"Look—we're at the road." Hope pointed to the big bur oak across from them. "I recognize the landmark."

Hunter reined the horse to a stop to gather his bearings before he guided Penelope onto the road and headed to their right.

"I sure hope this is a *gut* decision," he whispered for her alone after they'd been traveling for some time. He had plenty of doubts.

Hope never wavered. "It's the only decision. Conrad's survival depends on us getting hold of the sheriff."

He glanced over his shoulder at the people in the back and noticed something else. Two pen-lights of brightness. Headlights. Someone else was out on the road tonight. "We are not alone," he whispered.

Hope craned her neck to see through the back window. "I see them." She suddenly grabbed his arm. "Wait, the lights are gone now."

"What?" Hunter jerked around. The lights had disappeared. He believed the vehicle had turned off at Hope's home. It wouldn't take them long to realize Abe was gone.

They'd reached the sign announcing the shops up ahead. Hunter finally relaxed a little. "Almost there." Yet he couldn't help but feel the nightmare they'd gone through was far from over. "Once I make the call, we can use the communal barn near the shops to get the mare warmed up. It will be a *gut* place to wait for the sheriff."

The first shop emerged through the darkness. Penelope trotted along the frozen road surefooted, her coat blanketed in snow and ice.

Hunter guided the animal toward the phone shanty and stopped close. "Stay inside, where it's warm. I'll be quick." He got out and closed the door fast to keep the cold out.

The wind bit through his coat as he trudged the distance and picked up the receiver. There wasn't a dial tone. While panic took root inside him, he clicked the disconnect lever several times without any change.

Soon, the terrible truth became clear. The storm had taken out the phone. With a sinking feeling, he turned back to the buggy, where Hope watched him with an anxious expression. He hated delivering the news that they were on their own to survive.

As he struggled to come up with another way to save them, a far more imminent danger appeared down the road—headlights coming their way. There was no doubt in his mind it was the enemy.

Hunter ran for the buggy and got inside. "Someone's coming." Getting out of sight was critical.

"Were you able to reach the sheriff at least?" Hope asked while keeping her attention on the vehicle that was closing the space behind them. There was no way its headlights hadn't picked up the reflective triangle on the back of the buggy.

"I think they saw us. We must hurry," Hunter said. She deserved to know everything. "The phone is out. The weather probably knocked it and every other one in the county out." Hunter nudged the weary mare to a quicker pace.

Reaching the final building, he steered the horse around the corner to the alley behind the businesses. They drove by the storage building where his family kept their shop's damaged furniture. The communal barn became visible through the snow straight ahead. He reined Penelope to a hard stop. "I'll get the doors. Don't waste time getting inside." Hunter exited and ran for the entrance. He stepped aside while Hope drove the buggy through. Once the back cleared, he grabbed the first door and forced it shut. Before he could reach for the second, he spotted the vehicle creeping along the street in front of the shops.

Someone touched his arm. The alarm pouring through his body had him whirling toward the action. Hope. He almost doubled over with relief.

"Let me help you," she said. It took both of them to fight the gusts and close the door. Once secured, Hunter leaned against the frame.

"What do we do now?" Hope's worried gaze latched onto his.

"We stay put." Yet these men had proved themselves ruthless, and they'd seen the buggy. Knew he and Hope and the others were somewhere close. They'd search every possible hiding place until they found them. How long before they reached the barn? There could be no hiding the buggy. He had to think of something quickly to save their lives.

The structure had only a small window near the side door. Hunter peered through the ice-encrusted glass. "It's going to be impossible to see anything through this."

Abe and Naomi needed to know what they were all facing. "We have to tell them," he said and went over to the back of the buggy. Two sets of troubled eyes met his. "The phones are down and could be for hours, if not days. We won't be able to call anyone tonight."

The news brought fresh tears to Naomi's eyes. "My poor Conrad."

Nothing he could say would ease her fears.

Hunter tugged Hope out of earshot. "We're in trouble. It's only a matter of time before they come here."

Above the noise of the storm, another sound was far more disturbing. The vehicle. It was coming down the alley.

Hunter rushed to the window. Nothing but white could be seen through the frosty glass.

"We have to get everyone from the buggy and out of sight." He glanced around the space. Several square hay bales were stacked up almost as tall as himself. Beside them were a half dozen bags of feed. "Over there. We can use the bales as cover."

Hunter carefully assisted Naomi to the ground and nodded toward Hope. "Go with her. Both of you get out of sight." Hope clutched Naomi's hand and went over to the bales. She lowered Naomi down and crouched beside her.

If the men found the empty buggy, perhaps they would think its occupants had fled. A slim chance, but it was something.

Stubborn as always, Abe refused Hunter's hand. When the older man stumbled and almost fell, Hunter reached out to steady him.

"I am *oke*. I don't need you."

Holding back his anger was difficult. Hunter walked beside Abe and waited as he carefully lowered his frame down beside his *dochder*.

As much as Hunter hated the thought of having to use more violence to save their lives, he was almost positive it would come to that. He retrieved his shotgun from the buggy. As far as he knew, there were two men who had invaded his home and another person still at Conrad's home. There could be more. The shotgun wouldn't hold up against so many.

Near the side entrance, a noise captured his attention. Voices. His knotted stomach assured him there would be no avoiding a showdown with these men, and he felt ill-equipped to handle people willing to cause harm to get their way.

FOUR

Hope's heart felt as if it were ready to explode inside her body. Huddled close, *Daed* and Naomi stared at her with huge, fearful eyes. She did her best to put on a brave front she didn't feel.

Noises outside continued to grow louder. Where was Hunter? She edged close enough to see beyond the hay bale. Hunter suddenly materialized beside her, and Hope bit off a scream.

He ducked down and held her gaze. "They are coming inside."

A sharp breath slipped from her as she noticed the shotgun in his hand.

"In case they try to force us to go with them," Hunter told her.

She understood there would be no choice but to stand their ground. No matter what, they couldn't let those men take them. All their lives depended on their staying free.

The door creaked long and slow, grating

along Hope's frazzled nerves. A second later, what sounded like it slamming shut had her edging closer to Hunter.

"I thought you had it," a familiar voice growled. The uninjured man from the woods near Hunter's home. "That just about scared me to death."

"Look—there's the buggy. They're in here somewhere."

Quiet footsteps came closer. Hope's gaze found Hunter's face. He shook his head, warning her not to make a sound.

"This is Amish country. There are buggies everywhere around these parts." The familiar man derided his partner.

"Well, this one's got a horse attached to it. I don't think the owner would leave the horse harnessed to the buggy for who knows how long. Especially in this weather. I'm telling you, this is their buggy. They're here somewhere. Go see if they're hiding in the back."

Over her drumming pulse, someone shuffled closer. The bales were lined up parallel with the buggy's rear end. Once the man reached the back, all he would have to do was look to his left to see them hiding.

The man came into Hope's peripheral line of sight. She grabbed Hunter's arm and shrank against the bale. He was the one calling the shots at Hunter's home. The one who had threatened her and Naomi. He reached the buggy and peered through the back window.

"There's no one there." He turned slightly and stopped short, staring right at them. "Over here. I see them."

Hunter fired at the man who dived behind the buggy. The second man yelled something to his partner. Hunter leaped from his hiding spot and shot at the second man before ducking down beside Hope.

"We can't hold them off like this forever. There could be others coming. We have to find a way to subdue both men. Cover me," he told her and shoved the shotgun into Hope's hand when the first man charged toward them with his weapon pointed.

Hunter slammed into the man's frame and snatched at the weapon in his hand. The surprised man stumbled backward, slipped his finger on the trigger and fired. A shot flew past Hope and the rest of those kneeling.

"Get down," Hope warned, grabbing both her *daed* and Naomi. She pushed them low and covered them with her body while Hunter continued a struggle to incapacitate the gunman. Where was the second man?

"Get out of the way, Jerry, and give me a clear shot. We don't need him. We need her."

A crack of a weapon came from just beyond

Hope's line of sight. She jerked toward Hunter. The bullet barely missed him.

She had to do something before Hunter lost his life. Hope scrambled to her feet. The man shooting appeared surprised by her. She took advantage and fired a single round into the shooter's leg, her mark accurate. With a scream, he dropped his weapon and hit the ground clutching his injured limb.

Hope started for him. Dazed, the shooter seemed to remember his circumstances and scrambled across the ground for his lost weapon. Hope couldn't let him reach it. Leaping for the gun, she reached it before the wounded man. She shoved it inside her coat and pointed the shotgun at him. He slowly raised his hands into the air.

Hunter took advantage of the distraction and tried to get the weapon from the man. The two struggled back and forth, but Hunter ended up with it.

He shoved the man away and trained the gun on him. "Stay where you are. Don't try anything."

The man on the ground lost interest in his partner's struggle and clutched his wounded limb, his eyes spitting fire. "You're all dead, you hear me. Dead. He won't think twice about killing all of you."

It was hard to ignore the threat.

"Who are you talking about?" Hunter demanded while keeping watch on the man he'd disarmed. "What is this really about?" he prompted when neither man answered.

"You're not getting anything out of me," the disarmed man muttered.

"What about you?" Hope demanded of the injured man, who glared at her without answering.

Hope stepped closer. "Where is my friend? Where's Conrad?"

"You're wasting your time," the man said with narrowed eyes. "We're not going to tell you anything. Besides, the others will be here soon enough. And then it will be all over for you and your friends."

The threat shivered down her spine.

She eased back to the bales where her father and Naomi still hid. "Are you *oke*?"

Both nodded.

She moved closer to Hunter. "What if he's telling the truth and there are others coming this way?" she whispered. They had to act quickly. But the buggy would be no match for a car. How long before the rest of the men found them?

"Can you keep watch on them? I'm going to see if I can find something to tie them up."

"Go, I've got them covered."

Hunter looked to the closest man. "Don't try anything."

The assailant threw him a nasty look. Hunter hesitated before he started for the workbench by the smaller door.

Her *daed* came up beside her and took the shotgun. "I'll watch this one." He indicated the man standing.

Though weak from the beating he'd taken, and in a fragile state from the multiple strokes, her father was a protector by nature. He'd done his best to protect her mother from death even though he hadn't been able to defeat the illness ravaging her body. And despite the argument that happened between him and his *gut* friend, he'd tried to protect Hope from Hunter's betrayal. But he couldn't stop her heart from breaking.

"I found something." Hunter returned, carrying a length of rope. "It should be enough for both of them."

Hunter advanced on the man Abe guarded. He attempted to back away.

"That's far enough." Hunter grabbed one of his arms and pulled it behind his back. "Do you have him covered?" he asked her father.

"Jah." The word came out in a growl. Now was not the time to let an old grudge stand in the way of them living.

Hunter secured the man's arms, then knelt and tied his ankles together. Once he'd finished, he checked his pockets. "Where is your phone?" The man refused to answer.

Hunter came over to where Hope stood beside her father and Naomi. "Thank you," he murmured as he passed her *daed*. He turned to Hope. "Can you guard this guy while I tie him up?" He indicated the injured man holding his leg.

Hope didn't hesitate.

He knelt beside the man. "I need you to sit up."

"I can't move, much less sit up. You have to do something before I pass out."

While Hope didn't believe his injury was severe enough for him to lose consciousness, he had lost some blood. "Take some of the rope and tie it above the bullet wound," she suggested to Hunter. "It will slow the blood loss."

Hunter used his pocketknife to cut off enough to secure the bleed before he helped the man into a sitting position.

Once restrained, Hope examined the man's injury. "The bullet is still in there." She ripped off parts of her apron and covered the wound with it. "That should keep it safe until the sheriff arrives. We will have them send medical help for you."

"Wait—you can't leave us here!" he exclaimed when she moved away.

"You'll be fine," Hunter told him, and searched his pockets. "No phone." He faced the man. "Where is it?"

"Don't know what you're talking about." He stared Hunter down.

Hunter blew out a breath and indicated Hope should step away with him.

"The buggy will slow us down. We'll make better time by taking their car." He kept his attention on the man on the ground. "Neither man has the keys. They must be in the car still."

While the vehicle would be warmer, she had no knowledge of how to operate a car.

"Do you know how to drive a car?" she asked.

He smiled. Not like the young man who had won her heart, but still, it had the power to catapult her back to one of the most painful times in her life.

"I do—or at least I think I do. I can operate a tractor. The idea is basically the same." He glanced past her to *Daed* and Naomi. "We have to act fast for Conrad." The concern he had for his friend was there on his face. Hunter cared deeply. He'd fight for Conrad with everything inside him. He just hadn't cared enough for her to keep fighting for them. The realization hurt.

"I will check in the car. Maybe they left their phones there along with the keys."

Hope forced the heartbreak aside. "I'll keep watch over these two with *Daed*. Hurry, Hunter," she added because she couldn't get the man's words out of her head.

You're all dead, you hear me. Dead. He won't think twice about killing all of you. If that were true, then every second they wasted was one they might need to stay alive.

Hunter tugged his coat closer against a brutal north wind. The moment he stepped from the building, its strength blasted him full-force and almost knocked him over.

Bracing against it, he crossed the small space between the barn and the car. Forcing the driver's side door open, he looked inside. The keys hung from the ignition. *"Denki, Gott,"* he murmured while his head dropped with relief. A quick search in the console produced two cell phones. He grabbed one and tried to reach the sheriff's station. A fast busy signal was his only response. Landlines were down all over. He dialed 9-1-1. Same results. There would be no help coming from the outside. It was up to him and Hope to keep them all alive.

Hunter climbed inside and started the car. The two men had had the heat going. Hot air soon hammered his face, a drastic contrast against his frozen skin. Even the limited exposure could prove deadly in a short amount of time.

With the car running, he got out and started back for the barn. Other men were out there somewhere, searching for them and the young woman called Penny. Staying in one place for too long was dangerous, especially if the man's claims were true.

Hunter considered their options. With the car, there was a chance of reaching Eagle's Nest and the sheriff's station. If the storm hadn't made crossing Silver Creek impossible, there would be plenty of other issues along the way. Namely, the more than two-thousand-foot bridge over Lake Koocanusa. With almost whiteout conditions, neither option was a welcome one.

Hunter reached the back of the car and stopped long enough to adjust his hat down low on his head. Above the howling wind, another noise had him listening carefully. A thumping came from inside the trunk. It sounded as if someone were banging or kicking the lid.

All sorts of troubling answers followed him to the driver's side. Hunter popped the trunk and slowly eased to the back with the handgun pointed in front of him. Pulling in a quick breath, he looked inside and froze. He couldn't believe his eyes. A bound and gagged Conrad stared up at Hunter with a terrified look on his face.

"Conrad? You're alive." A second later, Hunter sprang into action. Tucking the handgun inside his coat pocket, he brought out his pocketknife and cut the ties from Conrad's hands and legs. "Let me help you out." Hunter reached for Conrad's arm. His friend shrieked and jerked away as if he'd been hurt. *They shot Conrad.* Hope's words played through his memory.

"I'm sorry." Hunter grabbed Conrad's other arm and assisted him from the trunk.

His friend was unsteady on his feet and stumbled against Hunter.

"How bad is it?" Hunter asked.

"Not bad, I think, but they would not let me have a look. Where is Naomi? Is she safe? I've been so worried about her and Hope. When they got away, I figured Hope would come to you for help."

"She's inside with Hope and Abe. All are safe." Hunter quickly explained about disarming the men. "*Komm*, let's get the others. We must leave immediately."

Staying close to Conrad, Hunter fought his way to the door.

"How many others are out there?" Hunter hoped Conrad could give him some idea what they were up against.

Conrad stopped with his hand on the door handle. "I'm not sure. There were several inside the house and more waiting in the SUV parked by the side." He opened the door and hurried inside.

Naomi and Hope turned.

"Conrad." Naomi's worried expression transformed to one of happiness when she spotted her *mann* standing beside Hunter. She ran into Conrad's arms weeping for joy.

Hunter stepped away to give them a private moment.

"Where did you find him?" Hope asked in shock.

"In the car's trunk." Hunter watched the happy reunion and fought back feelings of resentment. The type of marriage Conrad and Naomi had was what he'd imagined for himself and Hope at one time. They'd both made mistakes. Let their families pull them apart when the conflict should have brought them closer.

Stewing in regret was not a place he wanted to stay. He'd lived there too long. It was time to let the anger go. "I found the keys. Their cell phones were there, as well. I tried calling. It didn't go through. The weather must be affecting the cell service, too. But the car is running and it's warm inside. Let's get out of here while we still can."

Hope nodded. "What do we do about them?" She looked to the two men who had tried to abduct them.

"We'll put them in the buggy. There's blankets there." He told her about his plan to try to reach Eagle's Nest. "Once we are able to speak to the sheriff, his people can pick them up."

With Hope's help, Hunter got both men into the buggy and covered each of them with a blanket.

Hope's troubled gaze caught his attention.

"What is it?" he asked with a sinking feeling.

"I hear something outside," she whispered.

Hunter hurried out the side door with her. Above the wind and the hum of the car's engine came another sound. "That's a vehicle." He peered through the blizzard in the direction of the noise. Headlights penetrated near the community signs.

"We've got to get the car inside and out of sight." He hurried to open the swinging doors. It took both of them to pry them free again against the freezing weather. "I'll drive it in," he told her.

Hope slipped through the doors and went over to where her father and Naomi and Conrad watched.

Hunter quickly pulled the car into the barn.

With Hope and Conrad's help, he was able to get the doors closed again.

"There's another vehicle coming," he told his friend. "I'm going to see if I can cover the tracks left by the car."

He grabbed a broom leaning in the corner and slipped through the side door, not realizing Hope had come with him until he went to work getting rid of the tracks.

She took off her coat and used it to sweep the ground while keeping a close eye on the advancing vehicle. "Do you think the men somehow told them where we were?"

He'd wondered the same thing. "I sure hope not. According to Conrad, there are a lot of them. We can't fight them all." He glanced down at the roughly covered tracks. If they drove by, they might not realize anything had happened here. But if they stopped...

Hunter kept his misgivings to himself. "It will have to do."

Together they went back inside.

"I told you they'd come. You're all dead. You'll see," one of the men yelled from the buggy.

"If the vehicle stops close to the barn, these two will let them know we're in here." Conrad glared at the men.

He was right. They'd have to find a way to keep them quiet.

"Here." Hope handed him the scarf she had around her neck. "We can cut it in two and use it as gags."

Hunter took the scarf from her and realized it was the one he'd bought soon after he asked her to be his *fraa*. She still wore it. That had to mean something.

"Denki," he murmured when she looked into his eyes.

Hunter cut the scarf into two equal pieces. He handed Hope one half and advanced toward the injured man with the other. As soon as the man figured out Hunter's intentions, he began screaming at the top of his lungs.

The second man joined in. Hunter worked fast to secure the scarf. As he turned to silence the second man, Hope beat him to it.

While the two continued their muffled protests, the sounds of the vehicle grew closer. Doubts chewed at Hunter's brain. If they came down the alley behind the shops, would they see his and Hope's attempt to cover the car's tracks? As much as he wanted to believe they'd done a sufficient job, he wasn't convinced enough to put his life on it.

FIVE

They would be an easy target. Hope's mind went to work on ways to escape should those dangerous men venture this way.

She didn't want to share her fears with her *daed*. He had been through so much already. Hope went over to Hunter, who stood by the window trying to get a glimpse of what was happening, and told him her concerns.

He glanced past her to where the others stood watching the men. "You're right. If these two called their partners and told them about the barn, then they'll look inside."

Almost as if on cue, one of the cell phones inside the car began ringing. Hunter shot her a look before he hurried to the car and grabbed the phone. The call ended. The second phone rang. Cell service was apparently working.

Hunter turned both phones off and came back to where she stood. "I don't like it. Who knows what ways they have to find their missing people?"

Chill bumps that had nothing to do with the cold peppered her arms. Unfortunately, there was only one option. The two double doors in front of the barn were the only way to get the car out. "I have an idea." She told him they should get everyone into the car and unlock the two doors. If the rest of the men reached the barn, they could drive the car through the unlocked doors and get away. Hunter had backed the car inside, which would give them an advantage.

"But they will come after us. The car has snow chains on it, but I'm guessing the other vehicle is equally equipped. We need a way to disable their transportation. It will give us a head start at least."

She frowned as she watched him. "But how?"

"I have a way, but it will require you driving the car. Can you do it?"

Her stomach tightened. Once she'd helped her *daed* with the tractor. But that was only briefly, and this was life and death.

"I am not sure," she said honestly.

"*Komm*, I will give you a quick lesson. It isn't hard. This is an automatic transmission."

Hunter opened the door on the driver's side.

"You see that thin narrow pedal?" He pointed to the floor.

She saw the one he indicated. "*Jah*, I do."

"That's the gas pedal. You use it to go. The one beside it is the brake, for stopping. To go forward, you make sure the car is in Drive. To do that, you pull the gearshift down to the *D*. The *R* is for Reverse and the *P* is for Park." He indicated the gear shifter. "It's that simple."

She wasn't nearly as sure. "What do you have in mind?" Hope had a feeling she wasn't going to like it.

"If the vehicle comes this way, I will slip around behind the barn. I'm hoping they'll search all the buildings starting with my family's storage space next door. If so, it will give me time to grab the keys and disarm the battery cables when they go inside."

"You know how to do that?" she asked with a shocked look on her face.

Hunter smiled. "*Jah*. I picked up a few things while working on our old tractor. Anyway, as soon as I'm done, I'll jerk the two doors open and hop into the car. We won't have long to get away."

If they stopped at the storage building at all.

"What if they see you?" She wouldn't leave him behind.

"If they spot me, I'll head around to the front

of the businesses near the bakery. Get out of here as fast as you can. You can pick me up there."

It was a daring attempt and one that might end in Hunter losing his life.

"It is too risky. Perhaps if we leave now."

He shook his head. "They will see and follow us." He kept his attention on her eyes. "Hope, we have to try."

She stared at his handsome face and wondered if he was speaking of more than just their escape. But how could they try when they'd burned their chance at happiness to the ground?

She slowly nodded and whispered, "We have to try."

He squeezed her shoulder, his smile a knife to her heart. *"Gut."*

They returned to the window. Hunter cracked the door and listened. "It sounds as if they are close to the phone shanty."

"I'd better go. Get everyone into the car."

She grabbed for his arm when he would have left. Hunter stared down at her hand and then to her.

"Be careful, Hunter. These men won't think twice about hurting you."

His jaw tightened and he nodded before slipping from the barn.

"Everyone, get into the car." She told the people she cared about what was planned.

Conrad escorted Naomi and Hope's *daed* into the back seat.

Hope climbed behind the wheel and struggled to pull enough air into her lungs. She was so afraid. For Hunter. For them. For Penny. What if the men had already found Penny? She could be dead. They wouldn't want to leave any witnesses behind. She and Naomi and Conrad. Her *daed*. Hunter. They'd seen the faces of the two men inside, plus a third who was injured. Conrad could probably identify more.

Hope glanced back at the others, who watched her with fearful eyes. It was up to her to get everyone out of the barn and away before those men figured out Hunter had disarmed their vehicle. When that happened, they'd come out shooting.

Hunter slipped around the side of his family's storage building. The vehicle was turning toward the alley. He opened the door and left it standing ajar. Coming from the direction they were, he was certain their headlights would pick up the open door.

The vehicle made the turn. He slipped along the side and around back, then hurried down the space between his family's building and the barn.

Car doors slammed closed.

"Someone's been here. Our people told us they were coming to the place where the phone is near those businesses. Let's check inside."

Hunter peeked around the edge of the storage building. It wouldn't take them long to search the space. He left his protection and moved to the large SUV. A glance inside showed the keys were still in place. Clasping the door handle, he slowly opened it. The SUV's door squeaked and he froze, looking back toward the noise. When no one came running out, he grabbed the keys and released the hood.

As he moved to the front, he stopped. Voices inside sounded far too close. They'd finished their search. Hunter raised the hood and disconnected the battery cables.

They were coming out. He ran to the barn where Hope and the others waited. Hunter threw the doors open and jumped into the passenger seat.

"Go, Hope. Now."

She shoved the gear into Drive and hit the gas pedal. The car spun its tires, then flew from the barn. Hope grabbed hold of the steering wheel and jerked the car to the left without slowing down.

From his side mirror, Hunter spotted the men running after them with weapons in their hands.

"Get down, everyone." Just as the words cleared his lips, they were followed by rapid gunshots. The back window was hit. The glass shattered but held in place. More shots took out both side mirrors. Somehow, the shooters missed hitting the tires.

"Don't stop," he warned as Hope ducked and tried to keep the car in the alley.

She kept the pedal down and fought the conditions as they continued. Soon, the shower of bullets could no longer reach them and he breathed out a huge sigh.

"Is anyone hurt?" he asked the people in the back seat.

Conrad looked his wife over to make sure she wasn't, and Abe shook his head. "We are all fine."

"Did you get the keys?" Hope's voice was shaking. She and the others had gone through things that would break most people.

"I did, and I disabled the battery. They won't be going anywhere anytime soon." Still, he couldn't help but believe the men would find a way to come after them. "Do you want to keep driving?"

She immediately shook her head. "I was so

sure I would wreck us just getting out of the barn."

Hunter smiled despite the harrowing experience. They'd left the community shops behind. Hope gripped the steering wheel so tight, her knuckles turned white.

"Pull over the first chance and I will take over." His mind worked through the details of the route that lay ahead of them. There would be little chance of forgiveness for mistakes on the road to the bridge. One false move and they could die.

"Gladly," she said and didn't waste time stopping. Hope put the vehicle in Park and got out. They swapped seats in a matter of seconds and then were on their way.

Hope rolled the window down to look behind. "I don't see anyone. Still…" She shared his doubts. She raised the window and settled into her seat. "Do you think they'll get the SUV running again?"

He believed those men were resourceful, and none of them had bothered to disguise their faces.

"Probably." He peeked her way. "I don't think they'll give up and leave. They came here looking for Penny and have gone to great measures to find her."

The worry grooves between her brows deepened. "That isn't what I wanted to hear." She shook her head. "I keep thinking about Penny. If they find her…" She didn't finish, but he'd thought the same thing. Penny's life was in jeopardy.

Through the driving snow, something materialized ahead of them almost too soon to stop in time. Hunter braked hard, throwing everyone forward. Thankfully, they were all wearing seat belts. The car shuddered to a stop. Hunter leaned forward and focused on the object in the road with a sinking feeling. A huge bur oak had given way under the weight of the snow and ice. The road leading to Eagle's Nest—to freedom—was blocked.

"Stay here. I'll be right back." He shoved the door open and braved the storm because there had to be a way to get around it. If he could shove the tree from the road enough to make it through, they'd be okay.

Conrad got out and followed him to the massive oak. The road was completely blocked. There was no way they could move such a heavy object, and no getting around it on either side. They were trapped. It was just them against some very bad men he was positive they hadn't seen the last of.

"Without a chain saw or an ax, that tree

isn't going anywhere." Conrad confirmed his thoughts.

Hunter glanced around the frozen landscape. "Let's get back to the car. We need to keep moving."

Once inside, Hunter dusted snow and sleet from his coat.

"It's too big to move, isn't it?" Hope asked.

The sinking feeling settling into the pit of his stomach continued to grow. There would be no reaching the sheriff on their own and he had no way to move the tree.

He shifted in his seat. "It weighs too much, and we have nothing to use to cut it up."

She searched his face, obviously counting on him to find a way to save them, and he couldn't let her down.

"What do we do now, Hunter? We can't keep driving around. Eventually they will discover a way to start their vehicle. They'll find us."

Not to mention the car had a little over a quarter of a tank of gas. Under normal conditions, it would make it to Eagle's Nest without a problem. But these weren't normal conditions, and Hope was right. They couldn't keep driving around without a plan.

There was only one option that came to mind—his *bruder* Mason.

Mason was a former US Marshal who had returned to the Amish faith. Hunter, Mason, their *bruder* Fletcher and *gut* friend Ethan Connors assisted the sheriff and the county's search and rescue teams in finding those who went missing up in the mountains. Because of the work the Amish brothers did for the community and the county, Mason had been allowed to own a satellite phone and other emergency equipment, including a four-wheel-drive vehicle. He'd know what to do.

"There's only one option. Mason."

He waited for the response he expected, and it came quickly. "But that's on the other side of the mountains."

To reach Mason's farm, they would have to traverse a pass over rugged mountains that separated most of the rest of the West Kootenai community from the few farms on the other side. The road that crossed the mountains was narrow and not well maintained normally. He couldn't imagine what it would look like under these conditions.

"*Jah*, and it won't be easy." He glanced back at the people hanging on every word of their discussion. "But we have snow tires, so that's something. We can't give up."

When no answer came, Hunter put the car in gear and slowly forced it around on the road. The best way to reach the mountain pass was the main road leading into the community. With armed men looking for them, that was no longer an option.

Hunter worked through their options in his head. Some of the less traveled roads around the community were fine in good conditions but in this weather, he wasn't sure they'd make it.

"If we take the road right before the shops, we can connect with the mountain road after a little ways," Hope offered as if sensing his dilemma.

He'd considered it. The road was narrow and mostly used by the Amish buggies around the community.

"I know it's not ideal," she said when he didn't answer.

But it was their only real option. "It'll be fine." Still, he didn't feel very confident.

As they neared the shops, Hunter leaned forward and tried to peer through the blanket of white surrounding the car, but it was almost impossible. Had the SUV moved? They could be close. In these conditions, he wouldn't know it until it was too late.

SIX

The headlights penetrated the onslaught of snow just enough to see the road.

"Are those fresh tire tracks?" Hope studied the limited visual in front of her.

Hunter did the same. "They are."

"Those can't be ours. The blowing snow would have hidden them by now." The other option was terrifying.

"Let's get off this road." Hunter slowly turned the car onto the less traveled lane that would eventually connect to the mountain road.

The tracks were alarming. It meant the men who had been after them had found a way to get their SUV running again. Hunter told her he had the keys and he'd disconnected the battery. How had they managed to start the SUV without the keys?

Outside, the snow tires dug into the thick drifts but held the road. Hunter did his best to keep them moving forward at a safe speed. He periodically rolled the window down to check behind. Though the tire tracks had been ahead of them, Hope hadn't seen any further activity of someone driving down this road.

With no direct threat in sight, Hope went over every single conversation she'd had with Penny. Nothing in them gave any indication why armed men would be coming after her so relentlessly.

"What are we missing?" she asked under her breath. She looked over at Hunter. "There was nothing in my visits with Penny that made me think she was anything but a sweet young woman put in a difficult situation of having to raise her *sohn* alone."

"She never told you anything more about her husband?" he asked curiously, then gripped the wheel tight when the car hit a slick patch of ice.

Hope braced against the armrest while Hunter fought to keep the car on the road.

"Penny didn't say much about her husband's absence," she said once the car was under control. "Only that he was no longer in the picture."

"Maybe he passed away," Naomi reasoned.

Hope frowned and glanced back at her friend. "I guess it's possible."

"Or it could mean anything," Conrad said and drew his wife close. "Did she say where she came from originally?"

Hope ran through their conversations in her

head. "No, but I did see some grocery bags from a store in Eagle's Nest." That didn't necessarily mean Penny lived in Eagle's Nest. She might have stopped at the store to buy food on her way here. Hope looked to her father, who was staring out the window. "*Daed*, do you remember her saying where she lived?" Her father shook his head.

"Where is this house she's staying in?" Hunter asked with his full attention on the road.

Hope gave him the location.

He nodded. "I know the place. That farm isn't too far from Mason's home. It's been vacant for a number of years, though. At one time, there was an older *Englischer* couple living there. I think he passed away."

She remembered. "You're right. Several years back. I wonder what happened to the wife. I believe she lived there for a while by herself and then she was gone." Hope didn't believe she'd passed away—the news would have reached the community. "Maybe she moved? If so, how did Penny end up at the house?"

"She could be related to the former occupants," Hunter suggested.

She hadn't thought about it. "I guess it's possible, though she never mentioned having any ties to the area." Hope realized there were a lot of things Penny hadn't shared.

"Whatever her involvement is with these men, we can't leave a young mother and child alone with armed men looking for them."

He was right. They had to do everything possible to get to Penny before those bad men did.

Hope's thoughts flew over the details of the evening. When she'd awakened that Sunday morning, her thoughts were all about attending the biweekly service. It was one of the things that helped keep her grounded. The message given by the bishop had spoken of finding *Gott*'s purpose through every event in life. What was *Gott*'s purpose in this?

"Her *haus* is on the way, although it will mean taking a detour." Would the detour cost them all their lives?

"We'll get her and the baby." Hunter never wavered. "Somehow we'll make room for them in the car."

She smiled and squeezed his hand, so grateful. "*Denki*, Hunter."

He looked into her eyes for a moment before concentrating on driving through the monster storm. Even after his attention left her, Hope's heart refused to slow down. All because of what they'd been through, she told herself. Yet, being with Hunter like this had stirred up emotions she'd desperately wanted to believe had been laid to rest.

"Someone's coming up behind us." Conrad's tight voice interrupted her heartbreaking thoughts. "There are lights."

She and Hunter exchanged a surprised look before he rolled his window down.

"He's right." He shook his head. "I don't believe they followed our tracks." Not in these conditions. "Maybe they are searching all the roads around the community."

"What do we do?" she asked. If they didn't manage to avoid the SUV, they'd be facing a greater danger ahead. The road to the pass had a steady uphill climb coming up soon with dangerous drop-offs.

Hunter had no answer. "If we get caught on the mountain pass, it could be bad."

Hope's entire body tensed. She tried to remember the layout of the countryside beyond the snow-covered world facing them now. There was no place to get off the road and not get stuck.

"We can't outrun them," Hunter said as if speaking the question to himself. He killed the lights. "If we make it to the tee in the road, there's an old farmhouse that used to belong to the Millers. We'll have to get far enough ahead to reach it without being spotted. Otherwise…" He glanced her way. "I know it's a risk."

And there was a real chance the SUV's occupants would check the farm anyway. Still, their options were limited.

"Do it." Hope held on tight while Hunter picked up the car's speed. She glanced back at Naomi and her father. The trip had put a strain on Naomi she didn't need, and her father was injured.

"Hold on tight," she told them both. Conrad wrapped his arm around Naomi and gathered her close while *Daed* clung to the armrest, his eyes huge and troubled.

"We're *oke*." She sought to reassure the man, who had once been her world, of something she didn't feel.

Facing forward, Hope braced while Hunter pressed the gas pedal harder.

"We're almost to the tee," he warned. "This won't be easy."

Hope rolled the window down. "I can barely see the lights. You won't have long."

Hunter nodded. "Hold on, everyone."

Instead of stopping at the tee, Hunter kept going. He crossed the road and vaulted onto the drive leading to the house without slowing down.

Hope had no idea how bad the drive would be since the Millers had no living family members to keep it up. The place had been slowly crumbling to the ground for years.

Hunter clutched the steering wheel tight and kept the car under control while Hope checked behind them again.

"Nothing so far. They should be close to the tee by now."

Hunter kept driving. They passed the shell of a house and headed toward the family's old barn that had been sitting unattended for years.

"Should we put the car inside?" Hope wondered if there was any place to hide where the men wouldn't find them.

Hunter shook his head. "Too risky. We'd be trapped. I'll pull it off behind the barn. At least we'll have a way out if they come this far."

He reached the barn and drove around behind it to the opposite side. From where they were parked, the trees on the property would keep the car hidden from anyone coming down the drive. Unless they decided to search the property…

Hunter stopped the car and faced her. "I'm going to check to see where they are. Wait here."

She shook her head.

Hunter's jaw tightened. "Hope…"

"I'm coming, Hunter. You can't fight them alone," she stubbornly told him. Though he probably thought she was being headstrong— like her *daed*—she genuinely worried about his safety. What would he say if she told him this? Would he even believe her after what happened between them? She'd steadfastly held to her father's accusations and lost the man she loved.

As Hunter continued to stare into her eyes, something shifted. Was he, too, remembering their argument? The outcome of her decision? Did he still resent her for believing her *daed*?

A breath escaped her lips. Hunter broke eye contact and studied the whiteout beyond the windshield.

If she didn't find a way to put aside the past, it would end up taking everyone inside the car under.

Hope pushed the door open against the wind and got out. He did the same. Would there ever be a time when they could have a conversation without the past standing between them? At this point, it felt impossible.

Her first step had her sinking into the deep snow up to her knees. She pulled her foot free and stumbled her way around to the front of the car.

Hunter met her halfway. "Take my hand. I'll keep you from falling," he added when she stared at him with her mouth open. Hunter held out his hand and waited for her to accept it.

She slowly placed her hand in his. Holding his hand reminded her of the times she'd slip hers into his under the table as they'd sat across from each other at the youth singings, or during meals he'd shared at her *haus*. The times he'd walk her home and they'd shared their dreams together. Back then, everything was *oke* as long as she had him.

Hope forced the memories aside. Those two people were gone. Life's circumstances had changed them into the people they were today.

They reached the back of the barn and slowly moved to the side facing the drive. Hunter peeked out carefully.

"Do you see anything?" Hope asked from a few inches behind them.

"*Nay*. Perhaps they kept going."

She couldn't let herself believe it. The SUV had trailed them, but it hadn't been that far behind, and they'd had their lights on for a while.

It was impossible to hear anything over the gusts of wind. "We should take a closer look."

He nodded. With her hand in his, they stepped from the protection of the barn and straight into the teeth of the storm. The snow and ice hit them with enough force to knock them over. Hope hunched against the freezing wind and ice. Noticing, Hunter gathered her close for added warmth, for which she was grateful.

They struggled to the front of the barn while Hope couldn't get those angry faces from her head. The people following them were desperate to find Penny. Desperate enough to kidnap

Hope and her father—shoot Conrad and Hunter. They wouldn't give up. For whatever reason, they needed Hope to find Penny.

As she and Hunter neared the road, Hope spotted headlights through the storm. They ran for the dilapidated house, and to the far side, out of sight.

Hunter eased over enough to see what was happening. "They are heading straight for the homestead." He ducked back and pulled Hope along with him to the opposite side of the house.

"We have to get back to the others. If those men find them…" She didn't want to think what might happen to her *daed*, Naomi and Conrad.

"Conrad and your father will protect Naomi." Hunter slipped forward and looked around the side of the house. Hope leaned past him. The SUV was even with them. It crept along the snow-covered drive.

"If we cut across the drive and around the front of the barn, we should be able to reach the others before they are spotted," Hunter told her.

Moving through the thick snow was exhausting. Hope slipped several times and almost went down. Through it all, Hunter kept a firm hold on Hope's hand.

Before they had the chance to cross the drive, the headlights became visible through the storm.

Hunter tucked her behind a group of trees and gathered her close.

"They're coming back?" Hunter's astonishment matched hers. The SUV slowly eased past them.

"They didn't see the tracks." Hunter's relief was clear on his face as he watched the disappearing vehicle. "One blessing to come from this horrible storm."

Once the SUV's taillights disappeared, they crossed the drive and hurried back to the others.

Hope slipped inside the warmth of the vehicle while Hunter got in behind the wheel. Three sets of troubled eyes watched them.

"What happened?" Conrad asked.

Hunter told them about the SUV's close encounter. "We'll give them a little time to move on before we leave here."

Hope let the heater dissolve the cold from her limbs. The stories she'd heard about what happened to Hunter's family had seemed unbelievable until now. His sister-in-law, Victoria, had needed his *bruder* Aaron's help when she'd been hunted by members of her former CIA team. His *bruder* Eli's wife had almost died at the hands of a man who had once been part of her family. And then there was Mason. He'd been forced to protect his young *dochder* from horrible people who had wanted to kill the child.

Though all were safe now, their stories made her wonder how they'd found the courage to face such danger. Now, she understood. There was no other choice. When the lives of those you love are on the line, you will do whatever is necessary to protect them.

A chill that had nothing to do with the weather worked its way into her being. The bad things of this world could find their way into your life no matter how hard you tried to keep them out.

Even in this Amish community she loved dearly, where they chose to keep with the old ways and did not adhere to modern technology, bad things had a way of slipping in. Destroying lives.

Like the results of an argument between two old friends. It had destroyed a lifelong friendship, taking away Hope and Hunter's future.

No matter what had happened in the past, she wouldn't let this evil take Hunter's life. She'd brought this trouble to him.

He caught her watching him and she couldn't look away. Their eyes held. The good things between them came to mind. It had been a long time since she'd looked into his eyes and seen the young man she'd fallen in love with looking back at her. But that's what she saw now, and it almost reduced her to tears. Had she quit too soon on them?

* * *

"It should be safe to leave now." Hunter registered the unsteady note in his voice and dragged his gaze away from Hope's. When he'd been wakened from a restless dream what felt like a lifetime ago, he'd never imagined he'd be thrust into a terrifying getaway with the woman he'd once loved.

Hope hugged her arms around her body without responding. He put the car in gear and eased from their hiding place without using the headlights. Turning onto the drive, he wondered how he was going to make it down the driveway much less the treacherous mountain road they'd have to traverse without the lights. His hands held the wheel uneasily. But if he used the lights, he'd be driving the bad men right to their location.

A breath escaped. Tension coiled through his body like it would take control. He braked hard. There was no choice. He couldn't see anything. Hunter slowly flipped on the lights. The space in front of them illuminated, and nothing but white filled his vision.

Easing off the brake pedal, he gripped the wheel tighter as the car lurched forward. He tentatively pushed the gas. Despite the chains, the car slipped. The SUV's tracks had disappeared already. The storm continued to gather strength, becoming as much an enemy as those dangerous men.

By the time he reached the road's intersection, Hunter felt as if his hands were glued to the steering wheel, the muscles in his arms tense. He flexed them before readjusting his hold.

From the corner of his eye, he saw Hope watching him with a fearful expression on her pretty face. Since seeing her again, his emotions had been eating him up. He cared about her. Resented her. Wished he could go back to his simple unfeeling existence.

Hunter eased the car to the left. As much as he wanted to floor the gas and fly down the road, to get to the mountain pass and to Mason's as fast as possible, one false move could land them in more danger than they were in already.

"The road to the pass is getting closer." Hope's gentle words slipped past the terror in his mind.

Visibility was just a little beyond the hood even with the lights. Through the swirling white, the headlights caught something. A stop sign. They had reached the mountain road.

Hunter leaned forward and studied the ground through the illumination. The snow didn't appear disturbed, but he couldn't count on what his eyes showed him. By now, the wind would have blown snow over the tracks.

Puffing out a breath, he turned left once more. His bad feeling continued to grow as the road climbed. It would wind around the mountains and then back down through several smaller hills before reaching the valley. They'd grab Penny and the baby and head to Mason's home.

It sounded easy, but it was anything but. The danger standing between them and his *bruder*'s home wasn't just limited to the weather.

Even with the snow chains, the car was ill equipped for the conditions at the higher altitude. As he punched the gas and continued up the steep incline, the car slid to the right. Hope gasped and clutched the door handle. Though he couldn't see it, Hunter knew the road well. There was a steep drop-off on the right that would plunge them to their deaths.

He let off the gas. Tapped the brakes. They caught, but then the car slid backward.

Eventually the brakes held. With one foot on the pedal and the second on the gas, he managed to get the vehicle moving forward.

"That was close," Conrad breathed unsteadily. Hunter looked through the rearview mirror. Conrad held his wife close, his attention out the side window where the drop-off was a few feet from his view.

Hunter didn't answer but put his full attention on keeping the car moving forward.

As they continued traveling up the mountain, he couldn't let go of the uneasy thought. Where had the SUV gone?

Hope rolled her window down and glanced behind them, then ducked back inside. She brushed snow from her prayer *kapp*. "There's no one there. Perhaps they went back to the shops." If the driver had turned right, the SUV would eventually end up there.

Hope's doubtful expression confirmed she didn't believe it, either. He kept his thoughts to himself. There was no need to trouble the others.

They wound their way around a sharp turn in the road and something out of the ordinary captured his attention. A dark object near the side of the road.

"What is that?" he asked. His answer became apparent soon enough. The SUV was sitting on the side of the road.

"There's no way they won't see us," Hope whispered.

Hunter punched the gas because these men were not afraid to use their weapons.

As they drew level with the vehicle, doors opened and armed men jumped from inside.

"Everyone get down." Hunter didn't slow his speed. One man tried to open Conrad's door, but Hunter'd had the forethought to lock them.

When getting inside the car failed, the men opened fire. Hunter spun the tires in an attempt to escape. Bullets sounded like hail beating down on the car. If one wrong shot managed to take out a tire, or worse, the engine, they would be at the men's mercy. And there wouldn't be any.

The armed men ran after them shooting. At least the storm worked in their favor in that it kept them from being able to see the moving vehicle clearly.

Hunter reached the bend in the road and made it at high speed without swerving.

With his heart racing, he knew they had a matter of seconds before the SUV came after them.

They were almost to the top of one pass. The trip down would be faster and in many ways far more dangerous. Especially with men shooting at them. Without looking out his window, he was blind to what was coming up behind them, and it took all his concentration to keep the car on the ungroomed road with the snow piled up deep.

The wind whipped around the mountains, shoving the car violently. He was driving without any knowledge of how close those men were.

"Can you see anything behind us?" Hunter asked Hope without taking his eyes off the road.

"Hang on." Hope downed the window and stuck her head out. His answer came way before she responded when shots tinged off the back of the car.

She quickly ducked inside and rolled up the window. "They are gaining on us, Hunter. If they catch us up here…"

Though she didn't finish, he understood what was left unsaid. If they were forced from the road now, it would be a sheer drop-off.

They topped the mountain. It was downhill from here. One thought kept Hunter from panicking—the men needed Hope to find Penny. If they killed her, they wouldn't be able to track down the young *Englischer*.

Unless they'd found another way. If they had, they wouldn't need Hope alive any longer. The uneasy thought barely cleared his head when something slammed into the car and sent it veering toward the drop-off.

Hunter fought the momentum and was able to straighten the vehicle, but not before the car hit a glancing blow against the solid-rock mountain. It spun three hundred and sixty degrees while Hunter struggled to keep it on the road.

When he was finally able to right the vehicle, he rolled the window down in time to see the SUV struggling on the road. It spun sideways, and the engine stalled out. Men poured from the SUV and prepared to fire on them once more.

"They're disabled for now." Hunter punched the gas. They were heading down the mountain.

The car picked up momentum as it continued downward. Through his frantic thoughts, Hunter tried to recall the farms on this side.

There were only a couple of Amish places. He couldn't risk bringing their trouble to any of them. And if he kept going to Penny's, he'd lead the men right to her.

A couple of old abandoned farmsteads were scattered around the area. If he could reach one of them and get out of sight, it might be possible to keep those in the SUV from finding them. Let them get ahead before he tried moving again.

The car's speed picked up as they continued downhill. Hunter tried not to ride the brakes and get them hot. It might be impossible to stop if that happened.

Hope looked out the window and whipped toward Hunter. "They're coming after us again."

Keeping the car on the road was hard enough as it was. He didn't dare go any faster.

They were still some distance from the bottom of the mountain. And there was no way to get out of the SUV's deadly path.

He pressed the gas and the car flew down

the mountain, but not fast enough to outrun the SUV.

It slammed against the back bumper. Hunter fought with all his strength, but he was losing the battle quickly.

Please, help us. The simple prayer raced through his thoughts. A heartbeat later, the vehicle hit them again. Their car skidded on the slick road while the world around blurred past them.

Someone screamed. Prayers and moans mingled. The SUV struck them again before he had time to straighten the car. It flew from the road. Plunged down the slope. Branches scraping both sides was the worst sound he'd heard. The drop-off wasn't nearly as steep as Hunter had expected but every bit as dangerous. The deep snow accumulation hid dangers beneath its surface.

Brakes were useless. No matter how much he stomped, the forward momentum of the car wouldn't slow.

Hunter held on to the wheel and prayed they would stop before the harrowing ride claimed their lives.

Beside him, Hope clung to the dash and armrest. "We're going to crash."

Her panicked voice filtered through the fear in his veins. Like it or not, she was right.

Straight ahead, two lodgepole pines jutted tall against the sky. There was no way to dodge the trees. Steering the car was pointless.

"Hold on." Was there enough room between the two? He'd find out soon enough. The trees scraped the side of the car, the friction created enough to slow their speed somewhat. The car reached level ground. Hunter stomped on the brakes again. They finally caught and lurched the vehicle forward. It slowed, careening to the left. A huge snowbank did the rest. The car plowed into it before coming to a violent stop when the engine stalled out.

A long breath poured from his body. The frantic journey down the side of the mountain was over. His next thought was for the people in the vehicle. "Is everyone safe?"

He looked to Hope, who had lost all color. She slowly nodded through her dazed state. The three people in the back showed varying stages of shock. Abe struggled to speak. Conrad had his wife in his arms while Naomi wept.

"Is everyone *oke*?" he asked again in a bit harsher tone because he was worried. Naomi was pregnant. He needed vocal confirmation.

Conrad conferred with Naomi before answering. "We are."

Still, Hunter hadn't heard from Abe. The old man had already taken a beating. This couldn't have been easy for him. Abe forced himself to confirm while visibly shaking, his eyes huge and fearful.

Hunter tried to restart the car, but the engine wouldn't turn over. It was probably damaged beyond repair. That meant they were stranded here on the side of the mountain, and the men who had run them off the road were still out there somewhere waiting to finish the job.

SEVEN

Hope pried her hands free from the dash and forced the window down. She looked to the point where they'd gone off the road. The SUV was still up there. Probably trying to spot their damaged vehicle. How long before those dangerous men came looking for them?

Her heartbeat slowed enough to hear above its thunderous sound. When you first came off the mountain, there were mostly vacant farms. Farther down were a few Amish families, followed by several cattle ranches.

Hunter tried the engine again with the same result. "It's beyond what I can fix out here."

That meant they'd have to hike out.

"Doesn't the Hilty ranch have an additional barn over on this side? They keep horses they are training here, I believe."

Hunter was right. One of the largest Amish horse ranches in the state was owned by Elam Hilty. Elam and his family trained quarter horses for ranches across Montana. Though the family's main ranch was on the opposite side of the mountain, they kept some of the horses they were training here. It would provide a place to warm up. And maybe an extra buggy onsite.

"You're right, they do. If we can make it there." She stopped. For the battle-weary people in the car, trekking across the rough countryside seemed about as impossible to consider as what they'd gone through so far.

Hope worried about Naomi. "How are you doing?"

Naomi put on a brave face. "I am *oke*."

Her pregnancy was high risk and she'd been subjected to plenty of high-stress situations already. Now, she must traverse the elements once more. The heavy boots and warm coat would help. But would it be enough?

The mountain road wound close to their current location. Those in the SUV would be watching for any signs of the car or its occupants. The longer they waited, the more likely it was they'd be found.

"We don't have much time," Conrad said. "They'll search for us."

Hunter glanced back at his friend. "You're right. Even in the storm, there's a chance they'll find the car." Hunter opened his door and got out. While Conrad assisted Naomi, Hope went to her father.

"I can make it on my own," he muttered, yet he clasped her hand as he staggered to his feet.

"I know we're all tired, but we don't have a choice. Try to stay out of sight from the road." Hunter looked around at the weary faces and then to her. If only she could ask the meaning behind the gentleness in his eyes. But now was not the time for questions. Not when they were all fighting for their lives.

Hope linked her arm through her *daed*'s to support him, but he pulled free. "Not necessary, *dochder*, I'm not a feeble old man who can't walk on his own."

To argue would be pointless. Instead, she kept a close eye on him as he moved ahead of her and Hunter.

"It is *gut* to see some things never change," Hunter murmured.

Hope took offense. "He's not used to accepting help from anyone. The strokes have taken so much from him. His ability to get around on his own is one of the last things he has available."

Hunter's gaze softened as it slipped over her face. "That must be hard on you, as well."

Were they actually talking civilly to each other? Calling a truce after so long?

"It has been. Truthfully, he hasn't been the

same since *Mamm* passed." At times, Hope barely remembered the life they'd lived before her mother's death. Her parents had been married for more than twenty years when she died. As much as Hope tried, she hadn't been able to fill the hole left by her mother's death. "I love him. I would do anything for him." There was no other choice. Even when it cost her everything.

Her foot struck a downed tree limb and she stumbled. Hunter reached for her arm and steadied her. "Careful, now." His touch reminded her of the way he'd once looked out for her.

She pulled away because it was just too painful—this relationship that existed between them now. Whatever it was.

His jaw tightened but he didn't say a word.

Hope glanced back at Naomi. Exhaustion clung to the pregnant woman. Her footsteps were slow as she leaned against her husband.

"How are you feeling?" Hope stepped back to her friend and asked. With the baby's due date so close, she prayed the exertion Naomi had experienced wouldn't send her into labor.

"I am so very tired. I'm not sure how much longer I can walk."

Hope patted her arm. No matter what, they wouldn't leave Naomi behind. "You'll make it. We will help you."

Hope reached for Naomi's hand while Conrad clasped his *fraa*'s arm.

Up ahead, Hunter had caught up with her father. Neither spoke. Both stood rigid and proud. It was a glimpse into the past—Hunter resentful as her father blamed him for the wrongdoings of his father. Back then, *Daed* urged her to end her relationship with the son of a thief. She'd loved Hunter, but she couldn't defy her father.

"He is a *gut* man," Naomi murmured from beside her, and Hope turned her face to her friend. "It's a shame that things didn't work out between you. Shameful that what happened between your two fathers got in the way."

Hope looked away. "It was for the best. It showed me the truth. Hunter and I were not meant to be together."

Naomi kept her attention on Hope. Through the years, her friend had brought up the subject of the past between Hope and Hunter many times. Hope always did her best to steer the painful conversation to something else.

Hunter stopped suddenly and grabbed her father's arm. *Daed* was about to protest when Hunter put his finger to his lips and the truth became clear. He'd heard something.

He tugged her father into a thicket of lodgepole pines while motioning to the others to follow. Hunter shoved branches aside to reach the middle of the grove. Hope and Conrad got Naomi through the foliage.

"I heard an engine moving slowly up on the road," Hunter said in a low voice once they were all safely out of sight.

They were stuck in the middle of the blizzard and no closer to being out of danger than when they'd started this harrowing journey.

"Is it possible to keep moving?" Hope asked. All she could think about was getting Naomi out of the blizzard.

"We'll have to be quiet, but it's better than staying here and waiting for them to find us." He searched around the space. "If we stay in the trees, we should be able keep going without being spotted. The storm will cover any noise we make. Start walking. I'm going to see where they are right now. I'll catch up with you."

Hope turned to her father. "I'm going with him. You know how to reach the barn. Take Conrad and Naomi, and go. We'll be right behind you." He grabbed for her arm to stop her. "I will be fine. Keep moving, *Daed*."

Hunter was risking his life for them. She wouldn't let him do it alone.

He waited for her to catch up. "You should have stayed with your father," he said with an edge to his voice.

"Well, I didn't."

He slowly smiled at her answer. "No, you didn't."

They moved through the trees as quietly as possible. At the edge of the grove, Hunter stopped. She did the same.

Hope squinted through the blizzard, looking for the men. It was impossible to see much beyond where they stood.

He tapped her shoulder and pointed. Several people had entered the trees lining the road. So far, they hadn't spotted the car. With the weather, they'd have to be right on top of it to see.

"Let's go back," Hunter whispered close to her ear. "I'll feel better once we've put space between us."

Hope turned to leave. The motion put her inches from his tall frame and tossed her into the turmoil that was their past. She stepped back unsteadily. His hands descended on her shoulder to stop her from falling. She froze. Keeping the past at bay was hard when she was feeling vulnerable like she was right now.

Hunter let her go and turned away. Started walking. She dragged in a shaky breath and caught up with him.

Neither said a word. Exhaustion weighed her

limbs down. Yet it was the man beside her who dominated her thoughts.

They'd been so young when they'd first fallen in love. Perhaps too young to be prepared for a future together.

She and Hunter soon caught up with the others.

Her father turned as she neared. The worry on his face broke her heart.

"They haven't found the car yet," she told him in a low voice. "If we keep moving, we should reach the ranch before they can find us."

She couldn't help it—she looked Hunter's way. He said nothing to the two people beside him, yet his forehead furrowed.

Unexpected tears stung the backs of her eyes. Whatever happened between them was over and done, and the sooner she accepted it as final, the better. They'd both chosen their side and it couldn't be undone.

The trees thinned ahead of them. Hunter stopped walking to assess their location. Hope glanced behind them. Nothing but darkness and snow. A knot tightened in the pit of her stomach. She didn't understand anything about what was happening to them. And she worried about Penny. If these dangerous men were shooting at them—running them off the road—then did they still need to keep Hope alive, or had they found out where Penny lived on their own? Were Hope and everyone else with her now expendable?

Hunter stepped out into the open while fear worked its way down his spine. The wind slammed him hard enough to almost knock him off his feet. He turned to the road. Nothing visible through the trees. "Let's keep going," he told the exhausted group huddled nearby.

Hope hung back with Naomi and Conrad. He understood being with him had to be hard for her. He felt the same way. Whenever he looked at her pretty face, he remembered the way things had ended between them.

Hunter shoved those thoughts aside and peered through the bitter cold, almost too tired to draw another breath. They could be right on top of the ranch and he wouldn't be able to see it until it was a few feet away. A few yards in the wrong direction, and they'd miss it entirely. If they got lost in the storm, those men chasing them would be the least of their worries.

Abe stopped abruptly.

"What is it? Do you hear something?" Hunter asked him.

Abe craned his neck as if listening. "*Jah*, I do. It's the horses. They are uneasy."

The horses. They were almost to the ranch.

"Which way?"

Abe pointed to the left. "We almost missed it." The old man tossed him another angry look, as if to say it was because of Hunter's leadership.

Hunter followed Abe off to the left with the others. As they walked, Hunter picked up what Abe had heard—nervous neighs from the animals stalled at the ranch. The high winds must have them worried.

Hunter had been to the horse ranch a couple of times, mostly to buy horses for the family business. In the logging world, having dependable animals to pull the logs was key.

Out of the whiteness swirling around them, a fence post became visible. They'd reached the edge of the property. Elam's family had expanded to this side of the mountain when his reputation had grown beyond the Amish community he served.

"Which way from here?" Hunter asked Abe, who was a friend of Elam's father. They didn't have a world of time to be wasting.

"This way." Abe pointed. Hunter fell into step beside Abe while Hope caught up with them.

"Are we almost there? Naomi really needs to get off her feet."

Hunter saw her concern for their friend and nodded. "We are close to the barn." He glanced at Abe, who confirmed. "She can rest there and get out of the elements while we figure out what to do next."

On the occasions when he'd gone here with his *bruders*, he thought he remembered there had been an old buggy parked inside the barn. Was it still there? He sure hoped so.

Hope stayed close to his side as they walked the fence line. Every little noise had Hunter searching for trouble. His worst fear was that those men would appear out of nowhere and there wouldn't be time to get out of sight.

Something materialized among the white. The barn. Elam had prepared for the storm and had gotten the animals into the shelter.

They found the barn's entrance. Hunter quickly unlatched the door and ushered everyone inside.

Though still cold, they were out of the elements and the temperature was at least ten degrees warmer.

The barn was massive. More than a dozen quarter horses were stabled inside. Above the stalls, a small apartment was used for Elam's help to stay close to the animals. The last Hunter had heard, Elam was looking for someone to oversee this part of his business. Had that changed? If so, they would be putting another innocent life in danger.

Naomi looked ready to drop. She'd need someplace to rest awhile.

Hunter climbed the stairs to the apartment and knocked. When there was no answer, he opened the door and went inside. The apartment had a small sitting room and kitchen, with a bedroom and bathroom in the back.

He went downstairs. "There's an apartment up top. Naomi, you should rest for as long as you can."

Naomi's relieved face turned toward Hope.

She nodded. "He's right. It's been a difficult trip so far. You need to rest. For the baby."

"*Komm*, Naomi." Conrad placed his arm around his *fraa*'s shoulders and guided her toward the stairs.

"I'll come with you. Conrad, let me have a look at your injury." Hope turned to her father. "*Daed*, you should rest, as well."

Stubborn as always, Abe shook his head. "I'll be fine here in case I'm needed."

Hope's attention went to Hunter briefly before she and Conrad helped Naomi up the stairs.

A small bench sat against one of the walls. Abe made his way over to it and lowered himself down.

Though Hunter saw the old man at the bi-weekly church services and sometimes around the community, he'd never really noticed how frail Abe had become. His shoulders hunched against the burdens he carried. The strokes he'd suffered through the years had taken their toll. And Hunter had noticed a slight limp as he'd favored his left leg. On the same side, his arm hung against his body and his face slightly drooped, as well. Just a fragile old man wrapped up in his bitterness for something that happened years ago. It was a lesson to be learned. Live life to the fullest and don't let bitterness take control.

Hunter turned away, stuffing down the sympathy he'd never associated with the man who had caused so much damage to those around him.

A buggy had been shoved into the back of the structure. It clearly wasn't working properly. As Hunter neared, his heart sank. A missing wheel.

He took off his hat and slapped it against his thigh in agitation. Had they come this far—endured impossible circumstances—only to be stranded here in this barn? Though the property was located some ways from the road, there was a sign near the exit. If those men noticed, they'd come searching here.

Movement behind him had Hunter swinging toward it. Hope stood a few feet away.

"It doesn't look so *gut*, does it?" she murmured.

He studied her swaying frame. Hope seemed ready to drop, as well. Her prayer *kapp* clung to her head. Strands of wet hair peeked out. Those beautiful hazel eyes he'd fallen in love with were looking to him for assurances.

"There are a couple of wheels behind it. I don't know what kind of condition they are in." While most Amish preferred to use steel wheels now, this buggy had obviously been stored for a while, perhaps used for extra parts.

"Let me help you." She stepped close. Hunter ignored the distraction she presented and pulled out the first wheel. It had a wide crack running through it and would be useless. The second had a couple of spokes missing. If he could take two spokes from the cracked wheel and replace the missing ones, the buggy should be usable.

Hunter explained his thoughts to Hope.

"That should work," she agreed.

"Let's get them both over to the workstation." He guided the two wheels from the dark corner over to where a lantern sat on the workbench covered in tools. He'd contact Elam and explain what happened as soon as the danger passed. The optimistic thought hung in his head. So much stood between them and that happening. If they couldn't get the buggy working before those men showed up…

Hunter blocked the doubts and went to work removing the best two spokes from the cracked wheel while Hope assisted.

Having her close again was a two-edged sword to his heart. It reminded him of all the things they'd done together as youths and during their courting. Back then, he didn't much care what they were doing as long they were together.

After he freed the spokes, he went to work replacing the missing ones on the wheel they would use while Hope held it steady.

"How is Naomi holding up?" he asked because he was worried about his friend.

Hope met his gaze. Shock waves of wishful thoughts flew through his head before he dipped his head back to the work.

"She's anxious. This has been a difficult pregnancy as it is, but with what's happening now…"

He understood. The strain had to be severe on both *mamm* and *boppli*.

"I checked Conrad's wound. It appears the bullet didn't lodge in his arm, but he has lost a lot of blood." She glanced at his head. "How are you? That was quite a blow, plus the shot to your arm."

"I'm fine." He dismissed her concern for him. Conrad and Abe had suffered much more at these men's hands. And it hadn't mattered that Naomi was pregnant. They wanted to get to Penny, for whatever reason. He had no doubt once Hope led them there, they wouldn't think twice about taking her life.

"Let's put this wheel onto the buggy and get out of here while we still can. Unless they miss the turnoff for the ranch because of the storm, they'll check this place."

Her troubled eyes held his. "What can I do to help?"

Hunter gathered the tools he'd need and handed them to her while he rolled the wheel over to the buggy. Working together, they were able to get the wheel into place fairly quickly.

The buggy was enclosed, for which he was grateful. The thought of facing the storm again in an open buggy was not a welcomed one.

"I think I saw a driving harness over by the workstation. Help me move the buggy out of the corner."

They pushed the buggy into the open space.

Hunter spotted the harness and brought it over. "I really hate using one of Elam's horses without his permission, but we don't have a choice." Since Hope and Naomi had showed up at his house hours earlier, he'd done things he'd never imagined before to stay alive. Taking Elam's horse and buggy was just another to add to the list to repent for. Would his and Hope's efforts now be enough to save them? He sure hoped so.

EIGHT

"I'll get Conrad and Naomi. Can you help your *daed* into the back?" Hunter asked, his intense attention on her face.

Hope struggled for a calm she didn't feel. Being around Hunter like this was hard after the love they'd once shared. "*Jah*. Go and get them. I'll help *Daed*."

Hunter flicked a look at her father before he disappeared up the stairs.

Hope went over to her father, who sat with his eyes closed and head leaned against the wall.

The swollen lip and marks on his face had anger spreading inside her like a wildfire. She fought against the feeling that went against everything she believed in her faith. Forgiveness was key, but it was something she struggled with daily. She hadn't been able to forgive Hunter for choosing his father over her. She'd told herself she no longer cared, but being with him again had brought it all back. Part of her heart would always belong to him.

Daed's eyes snapped open as she neared. She forced the troubles of her heart aside and smiled. "How are you feeling?"

He kept his attention on her face. "Better. You are hurting."

She shook her head and tried to deny it. "No, *Daed*, I'm fine."

"*Nay, dochder*. He hurt you again."

Hope dropped her gaze. How could she tell him it was *he* who'd hurt her?

"It was no more his fault than mine. We both agreed to call off the wedding. It's just spending so much time with him again. But I am *oke*." She told him she would help him into the buggy.

Her father's usually stern expression softened. "You are so much like your *mamm*." He stood on his own. "At times, I forget she's been gone almost six years now."

His slow, labored steps were a constant reminder of the things *Daed* had suffered through since his *fraa*'s passing.

Unexpectedly, he turned toward her and placed his hands gently on her shoulders. "Perhaps I was wrong."

Her eyes grew large. She had no idea what he was talking about. Before she had time to ask, Hunter returned with Naomi and Conrad.

Her father used the step to climb inside while Hope stared after him.

Conrad assisted Naomi into the buggy and followed.

Hunter and Hope went around to the front. He waited while Hope stepped up.

"I'll get the barn door," he told her, but didn't move. She could feel him watching her, sensing the turmoil churning inside. He'd always been *gut* at knowing what she was feeling.

"Did something happen?"

Hope slowly faced him. The compassion on his face had her drawing in a steadying breath. It reminded her of the Hunter she had loved.

She shook her head. "Just worried." Hope grabbed onto the first excuse that came to mind. Her emotions were all over the place. *Why couldn't you have fought for me? Why didn't I fight for you?*

He kept his attention on her for a moment longer before he moved away to open the doors.

Hope directed the horse from the structure. The storm had grown in strength since they'd entered the barn. It felt as if they would forever be covered in white.

As soon as the doors were closed, Hunter climbed into the buggy, and Hope handed him the reins. She tried to control the chaos inside her heart.

Perhaps I was wrong. What had her *daed* meant by those words?

"The snow is too deep to go cross-country. We will be forced to take the road."

The knot in her stomach tightened. Taking the road would mean they would be exposed. Those men were still out there somewhere, searching for them.

Unless they'd found Penny already.

She was missing something. How could a sweet young girl like Penny be associated in any way with such dangerous men?

After she and Penny first met, Hope had followed Penny to her home so she would know how to reach her. They'd gone over what would happen next. During that time, Penny had constantly checked the windows, as if expecting someone to show up.

"She wore a wedding ring," Hope said unexpectedly.

"Who did?" Hunter asked with a frown.

"Penny. She still wore her wedding ring." Did it mean anything? Perhaps she and her husband had recently split up.

"You think she wasn't telling the truth about her husband not being part of her life?" Naomi asked. "But why?"

Hope looked her way and shook her head. "I do not know. Perhaps I'm trying to make sense out of something that doesn't. I just can't see any of those men being her husband. I don't think she's running away from him."

"But she was obviously troubled by something."

Hunter was right. The numerous trips to the window. The startled looks whenever she heard any strange sound outside.

Hope watched the road ahead through the window. "Maybe they hurt her husband." If Penny had witnessed those men harming her husband—or worse—it would certainly explain why she would want to disappear into the remoteness of the West Kootenai community.

The horse kept a steady pace while her thoughts spun to dark places. She knew bad things happened no matter how strong your faith, still, it was hard to accept that someone as sweet as Penny had been part of something deadly.

"How is your father doing?" Hunter asked quietly, drawing her back to the present.

Hope's eyes widened as she looked at him. His concern was unexpected. The animosity between *Daed* and Hunter had been evident since they'd found her father on the floor at her house.

She looked over her shoulder to where *Daed* sat with his eyes closed. The marks left by his attacker's fist were hard to witness. "As *gut* as he can be, I guess. He's been through so much already. He didn't deserve this." The left side of *Daed*'s body had been permanently damaged by the last stroke. His doctor put him on medication that he sometimes forgot to take. And she didn't know what she'd do if she lost him.

Hunter reached for her hand and clasped it. "I'm sorry."

She swallowed several times, but words wouldn't come. At one time, Hunter had loved her father, too. *Daed* called him his *sohn*, expecting one day Hunter would be the son he'd always wanted.

And then the argument happened.

"I am so afraid the next stroke will be the one…" She couldn't say the word. She lived with the fear of losing her father. Hope couldn't imagine her life without him.

He squeezed her hand. The strength of his touch seeped into her, making her feel stronger. But he wasn't hers to lean on anymore.

Hope pulled her hand free and stared straight ahead while her heart crumbled.

"Where are those men?" she wondered aloud. After showing such determination by breaking into Hunter's home and pursuing them relentlessly, she couldn't believe they would simply give up now. After all, she and the rest of those in the buggy had seen their faces and could identify them.

"They could still be searching for the car."

But his words were not spoken with confidence. "You don't really think so, do you?"

He shook his head. "No, I don't. The less time we are on the road, the better." Hunter sat forward, his full attention ahead as the road wound around another set of lesser mountains. She glanced down at the drop-off on her side and shivered. They'd barely survived the last one.

Driving snow continued to bombard the horse and buggy. They were still some distance from Penny's home. With visibility nonexistent, it felt like it would take forever.

"I don't see any tracks." The tension became clear in Hunter's tone. "Still, if they already came this way, we probably couldn't tell."

A sweeping bend approached. Hunter eased the horse into the curve.

"I see headlights," Conrad leaned forward and said.

A glint of lights in the distance behind them caught Hope's attention.

Hunter whipped around. "We have to get off this road. Now." His breath burst out.

The only option was taking the gelding to the left to avoid the drop-off on the right.

"Over there." Conrad pointed to a level spot off the road. It was wide open, but if they could get far enough away, the men in the SUV might not see them.

Hunter guided the horse carefully from the road into deep snow accumulated at the side. The animal stumbled down the ditch, then plodded forward until they could no longer see the road through the snow. Hunter pulled back on the reins. The animal stopped.

Hope's heart beat off every second they waited for the enemy while she craned her head toward the road. "They should be here by now." Had they spotted the buggy and killed the lights so they could attack without warning?

"I don't like it," Hunter told her. "I'm going to check it out." He reached for the handle, but she grabbed his arm once more.

"I'm coming with you." She waited for him to refuse. As they stared at each other through the small space separating them, there were so many things she wished she could ask about, but it was not the right moment. Would there ever be a right moment?

Hunter opened the door and hopped out.

"Do you still have the shotgun?" she asked her *daed*.

He held the weapon up.

"Gut." Hope handed Conrad her handgun.

"Just in case." She left it at that and jumped down beside Hunter, the deep snow cushioning her dismount.

"Stay close to me," Hunter whispered. The tension woven into those simple words set her nerves on edge.

She reached for his hand. To keep steady, she told herself. Truth was, if he was close, she felt safe.

After only a few steps, their coats were covered with snow. It clung to everything—even her eyelashes—making it difficult to see.

At the bend, Hunter peered down the road toward where she'd seen the lights.

"There's nothing there."

Hope learned past him. "Could they have stopped to look for us?"

"It's possible, I guess." He faced her. "Let's keep going."

With her hand in his, they crunched over the frozen ground. The road wound around another curve on the opposite side.

Still nothing.

"Maybe we should head back. We might be able to reach Penny's place before they see us."

Hunter didn't move. "They were not this far behind us." A chill worked through her body. She understood what he meant. "Let's walk to that next curve."

They'd taken only a couple of steps when Hunter stopped. A breath later, she spotted the SUV sitting on the side of the road with its lights off. He hurriedly tugged her out of sight.

"What are they doing?" she whispered.

"I don't know. Maybe they stalled out. Let's head back to the others. If they are stuck, it will give us a head start."

"Hunter, look." Another set of headlights shone from the road above the SUV. "Someone else is out here. This is bad," the words slipped past her frozen lips.

Another *Englischer* was on the mountain and whoever was in that vehicle could be in danger.

"We have to get out of here before this thing blows up." Hunter watched the second vehicle make its way toward the SUV.

Hope didn't move. "What if they are in danger?"

He understood her fears, but they wouldn't be able to help the people in the second vehicle if they were shot in the process. Their best course of action was to get the police involved.

Hunter noticed several men exiting the SUV.

"They're coming," one of them said. Hunter recognized the voice from his home.

"I heard something in those trees," another man said. A flashlight flipped on. Hunter tugged

Hope into the woods along the road. The flashlight beam struck far too close.

"There's nothing there." The first man sounded angry. "Come on. They're coming."

"No, I'm telling you, I saw something move." The second man wasn't giving up.

"He saw us," Hope whispered close to Hunter's ear.

They had to get deeper into the woods before the man caught them in his flashlight, but this was dangerous territory. At the foothills of the mountains were places where one false move could result in a fatal fall.

The flashlight continued to gain on them. Hunter grabbed Hope's hand and ran while praying they wouldn't be plummeting to their deaths.

"There *is* someone. Over there." The flashlight hit them dead-on. "It's those Amish people. The midwife and the other fella. They survived the crash."

Fearful they'd both take a bullet to the back, Hunter kept running with Hope.

Her hand was pulled from his. Hope screamed. She was gone.

"Hope," he yelled.

Footfalls thundered his way. He had to find her.

"Hunter, help me. I'm going to fall. I can't

hold on much longer." Her frantic voice reached up to him. He stopped short and realized a sheer drop-off was inches from his feet. Hunter peered through the snow and saw Hope hanging on to a decaying tree branch a few feet down.

If she fell…

To her right was a narrow ledge on the other side of the tree.

Time was up. He had no other choice. Hunter leaped toward the ledge and prayed he wouldn't miss it. He landed hard and slammed to his knees on the ground. Ignoring the pain, all he could think about was Hope.

He grabbed her wrist. "I've got you. I won't let you fall. Can you put your leg up over the tree trunk? Hurry, Hope. They are almost here."

With him gripping her wrist with both hands, she struggled several times before she managed to swing her leg over the trunk. Hunter dragged her the rest of the way up beside him. His arms wrapped around her, and he got them as low as possible. The branch she'd been holding on to snapped and fell to the ground below. If he'd been a few seconds later…

Hope clung to him. He'd almost lost her. While his heart raced over what might have happened, a new threat reached them. The flashlight beam searched the place where Hope had been moments earlier.

"Where'd they go?" the determined man asked.

A second flashlight bounced all around, coming close to where they squatted.

"I don't see anyone. Are you sure they went this way?" This was the first man.

"Yeah, I'm sure."

A light pinpointed the drop-off. "Well, if they did, they're dead now. Too bad. She knew where Penny is hiding. He's not going to be happy."

Hunter couldn't believe how ruthless these men were. The flashlights continued to shine all around.

"Come on. Let's go back to the SUV. Once he arrives, we'll get Penny's hiding place out of him. One way or another."

Hunter's gaze fastened on Hope's. He could feel her trembling in his arms. What was this man talking about? An uneasy feeling took root in Hunter's stomach.

Snatches of conversation faded, making it impossible to hear.

Hunter eased up a little so he could see the ground above. The men's flashlights were moving in the opposite direction.

"They are heading back to the SUV. We have to reach the buggy and get to Penny before they find her."

Hunter scrambled up through the ice and snow until he was on solid ground again. He held out his hand. Hope grabbed it and he pulled her up beside him. "It's not safe to go back using the road. We'll have to be careful. I don't want to risk falling down another drop-off."

With his arm around her shoulders, they started walking at a fast pace. "That was terrifying," she whispered, her trembling voice confirming her fear. "I thought I was dead."

Hunter tugged her closer. He had, too. The image of losing her in such a horrific way was a slap-in-the-face reminder that he still had feelings for her.

He stayed at the edge of the woods until they were some distance from the SUV.

"This should be where we left the buggy." They were parallel with the spot where he'd stashed it.

"Who do you think they're waiting for?" Hope asked. "Who else would know where Penny is hiding?"

"Whoever it is, if they find her before us, she's in trouble. And if there is someone else who can tell them where she lives, then they no longer need us." He let go of her hand. "Wait for me here. I want to see if they're still parked."

He edged toward the road. The second vehicle had reached the SUV. He watched it pull in behind. Headlights were shut off. Doors opened and closed. Voices carried his way. The expected attack didn't happen. Conversation continued. One of the men laughed. The men in the two vehicles obviously knew each other. The thought settled uneasily around him.

It was time for them to leave, no matter what was happening. Hunter returned to Hope. "They aren't trying to carjack the second vehicle. They know each other. This has to be the person who can lead them to Penny."

Hope's shocked gaze held his. "This is bad. She doesn't have much time."

They crossed the road and started for the buggy, fighting the wind every step of the way.

"I can't imagine why they are doing this," Hope said, her thoughts mirroring his.

"Whatever it is, it must be worth enough to them to harm others. I have no doubt they will kill anyone who gets in their way and can identify them."

Though walking blindly through the storm, he believed the buggy was close.

"I see it. Over there." She pointed.

He caught a glimpse before the wind swirled the snow and it was gone again.

"Denki, Gott." He barely had the strength to get the words out, but they came from a grateful heart. Hunter released a frosted breath into the air and started toward the buggy. The sooner they got to Penny's, the better. The horse

neighed as they approached and he got wind of them.

Hunter forced the door open and helped a frozen Hope inside.

Three concerned sets of eyes watched them.

"What happened? We were worried they had you," Conrad said.

Hunter did his best to explain their ordeal. "There's another vehicle. And we overheard one of the men saying they had someone else who knew how to find Penny."

Hunter shook the reins, and the gelding trudged toward the road.

On an impulse, Hunter tried the cell phone again. Another fast busy signal. He turned it off and stuck it back into his pocket.

"I just want this all to be over," Hope murmured beside him, rubbing her temples. Exhaustion clung to her beautiful face.

The anger and resentment he'd carried so long for her melted. "I'm sorry you've had to go through this."

Hope shifted toward him and searched his face. "*Denki*, Hunter." She swallowed several times before she said, "I know things have not been *gut* between us in a long time, but you were once my friend, and I'm grateful for your help."

Friend. It hurt to hear. More than once, he'd

wished he could go back to the time before that incident happened between their fathers. Maybe he could change things between them. Save his relationship with Hope.

"It was the right thing to do," he murmured and turned away. He kept his attention on the path ahead. *Friend.* The word left a bad taste in his mouth.

The horse struggled to traverse the deep snow.

"There's the road."

He registered the unsteady tone in her voice.

Hunter guided the gelding onto the road once more. He scraped the damp hair from his forehead beneath his hat. With the weather, it would take twice as long to reach Penny's home. Did they have that much time?

"The one thing we have going for us is we have a better knowledge of the countryside," he said, almost to himself. "Even if they do know where Penny lives, I'm guessing they aren't from around here. Chances are it will be harder to locate Penny's place, especially in this storm."

Her brows shot up. "You're right. There's no way they can find Penny before we do." She reminded him of the old Hope—always so positive. Never seeing the downside of a situation. That was why what happened between them had been so surprising. He'd thought at some point she'd come around and see the truth—or at least *his* truth. Yet she had held strong to Abe's belief the Shetler family had wronged him. Maybe if he'd been more willing to listen to what wasn't being said? Maybe he'd have realized both Hope and Abe were still suffering from the loss of Rhoda. If he hadn't been so caught up with his own anger and resentment, he might have seen that, backed off and given them both space.

His shoulders slumped. What *gut* did it do to think about the past? He couldn't change it. With armed men coming after an innocent woman, he had to stay focused on the present. He thought about what little information they knew about Penny. Anything to keep his mind off their heartbreaking past.

"Do you all mind if we go over what we know so far?" His question surprised her. "I know it's a long shot but maybe there's something you've forgotten, or something Naomi and Conrad or Abe will remember that might help us figure out what's really happening."

Hope shifted toward her father. "Did those men say anything to you beyond wanting to know where I had gone?"

Abe's gaze shot between his *dochder* and Hunter. The marks left by ruthless men were a reminder of how far they were willing to go to get what they wanted.

It made him sick to think of someone picking on an old man. Despite Abe's crankiness, he didn't deserve what he'd gone through. At one time, he and Hunter had been close.

"They barged into my *haus* angry and spitting fire, demanding to know where you'd gone. One snatched me out of bed and started beating on me when I wouldn't tell them." He shook his head. "But I do remember something I'd forgotten before. One of them mentioned money. Not the one beating me—the other one. He said something about how this went beyond what he was willing to do for money." Abe shook his head. "The man beating on me got really mad. He told him to shut up and help, but he didn't. Just stood by the door and didn't watch."

At least one of the men had a semblance of a conscience. Not that it mattered. The rest were stone-cold bad.

NINE

Was it possible everything they'd gone through had been about money? Hope couldn't imagine doing such horrible things because of greed. They'd hurt innocent men who hadn't done anything wrong.

"Did they say anything else?" she asked her father. Every time she looked at his face, anger burned within her. He could have suffered another stroke, or worse.

"The one man looked too afraid to speak. The other was too busy beating on me. I thought he would kill me and so…" He hung his head. *Daed* had given them what they wanted.

Hope squeezed his arm. "I'm glad you did."

"The man who beat you sounds like the one calling the shots," Conrad told them. "He was furious when the others came back without Hope and Naomi. He pointed the gun at my head and demanded to know where you would go for help. I told him about the phone shanty."

He stared down at the floor. "I had no idea I would be leading them straight to you. Yet, if I hadn't, I might have died."

Conrad's words drove home how dangerous these men were.

Past the weary faces of the passengers in the buggy, Hope caught a glimpse of something through the blizzard. "Oh, no," she whispered.

Hunter turned.

A single vehicle coming their way. Through Hope's panicked thoughts, she tried to think of someplace safe for them to hide. Their only choice was the woods near the road.

While Hunter guided the horse toward the trees, Hope kept her attention on the advancing lights.

"They are going way too fast," Hope murmured. The vehicle flew down the road despite the conditions. At that speed, it wouldn't take long before they reached the buggy.

As the vehicle continued closing the space between them, the buggy reached the trees.

"Do you think they saw us?" Hope asked.

Hunter kept the horse moving away from the road. "I sure hope not."

Headlights illuminated the place where they'd been.

"Please don't stop," Hope whispered. The

lights went a little way past the spot and stopped. "They saw us. Hunter, we have to keep going."

Hunter shook the reins. The weather-weary animal trudged forward.

Through the headlights, Hope was almost positive she saw movement.

Before she could get the words out, the woods near the movement exploded with gunfire.

"Get on the floor," Hunter shouted above the noise.

The three people in the back hit the floor. Hunter grabbed Hope and tugged her down low with his body covering hers. Bullets blasted large holes in the fiberglass of the buggy.

It felt as if the shooting would never end. The gelding, frightened by the barrage of bullets, charged through the woods. A new fear became far too clear. Recent fires had left dozens of downed trees scattered around. One wrong step by the animal and it would be over.

Hunter returned to the bench seat and wrapped the reins around his hands. Hope scrambled up beside him as he did his best to control the animal while the shooting continued. By now, they were out of range for a direct hit. Still, calming the panicked horse wouldn't be easy.

"They know we're still alive." Hope realized those men wouldn't stop until they'd taken care of every single person in the buggy.

"They are coming after us," Conrad yelled over the noise.

Hope looked through the back window. The SUV had entered the woods behind them. Even at the horse's pace, they couldn't outrun the massive vehicle.

Hunter held on to the reins and did his best to control the animal. The gelding stumbled once but avoided losing its footing.

"Hunter, they are gaining on us." Hope watched as the SUV continued to plow the ground between them.

"Everyone, move to the front of the buggy in case they strike us from behind. The buggy wouldn't hold up to such a blow."

Conrad gathered his wife and Abe, and moved them as close to the bench seat as possible.

A second later, the SUV slammed the buggy. Hope screamed again. The back all but disintegrated. Pieces of fiberglass billowed in the wind. Snow flew through the gaping hole left in the vehicle's wake. As Hope continued to watch in horror, the driver prepared for another attack.

Her father grabbed the shotgun and moved closer to the opening.

"No, *Daed*!" Hope shouted, terrified he would be killed.

Daed ignored her and shot, the sound reverberating through the space. Her father's aim was accurate. He'd struck the front tire. The SUV swerved hard as the driver fought to keep the vehicle from turning over.

The horse continued to gallop while the SUV's driver finally got it under control.

They'd survived the attack. "Thank you, *Gott*."

A breath later, doors opened and the armed men poured out, firing once more.

Everyone in the buggy ducked. The gelding panicked again and picked up speed. Shots struck every part of the buggy. One hit the wheel spokes. The wheel wobbled precariously. Hope was terrified it would come off. If it did, the buggy would turn over.

Hunter forced the gelding to a slower speed. "We can't afford to lose that wheel," he murmured while the men continued firing. "We've got to get someplace safe to fix it."

If they lost the wheel, the buggy would be useless. They'd be on foot. And their only chance at escaping would be taken away.

Thinking beyond the moment and the danger facing them was hard. Many of the houses on this side of the mountain belonged to *Englischers*, like Mason's friend and business partner Ethan Connors. But they wouldn't make it to Penny's place on the damaged wheel, much less to Mason's or one of the ranches.

"There are several old abandoned farms coming up," Conrad reminded him. "Perhaps one of them will have the necessary tools to fix the wheel."

Most of the homes Conrad mentioned had been vacant for years. The owners either passed away or moved on. Still, it was their only option. Once their attackers got the SUV's tire changed, they'd keep coming.

"The first one's going to be on the left side of the road," Conrad told him. That meant they'd have to go through a ditch to cross the road with a vulnerable wheel that could leave the buggy at any time.

Hunter directed the horse toward the road. "Where's the second car?" He voiced his fears aloud.

Hope turned troubled eyes his way. "I only saw one set of headlights. Do you think they turned back?"

He didn't believe it. If the second vehicle was on the road, they would be heading right for it.

"How far before we reach the first house?" Hunter glanced back at Conrad.

"Maybe a couple of miles."

"You think the second vehicle will be watching for us." Hope read his thoughts.

He looked straight at her. "I do. We won't survive another attack. Even if we are able to get the wheel fixed, the buggy's in bad shape."

A visible shiver ran through her frame.

Hunter kept their speed at a crawl while remaining in the woods close to the road.

"You are almost there," Conrad warned. "If you don't hit it just right, you might not be able to find the place in the snow."

Hunter pulled in a breath and halted the gelding. "I'm going to check before we cross. I want to see how bad it is."

He wasn't surprised when Hope climbed down beside him. Though he hated putting her in danger, Hunter was happy to have her with him.

He moved to the wheel and checked. The spoke was almost completely shattered into two pieces.

"Do you think it will make it?" Hope's brow furrowed. She had doubts, as well.

"It's bad," he told her. "We'll have to go slow." With her at his side, they edged to the tree line. Hunter barred her from going out when something caught his attention. A sound. He tugged her from sight.

"What is it?"

It took him a second to realize what he'd heard. The crunch of tires on the ice-encrusted road. "It's got to be the second vehicle." But there were no lights.

Hunter clutched Hope close and hid behind a tree. The car eased closer. Had he gotten the buggy out of sight enough? His doubts raged while the car crawled along the road. Someone had rolled a window down and was shining a flashlight around in the woods.

If they were spotted, it would be all over. The flashlight beam hit the trees where they were standing, bathing their surroundings in light. The car slowed. Hunter held his breath and prayed. A second later, the flashlight moved to the next group of trees as it continued its slow movement.

When it was some distance away, Hunter let her go and stepped from his hiding place. "As much as I want to get the buggy across the road, I'm worried they'll come back." He didn't know what to do.

"I'm guessing their friends in the SUV told them to look for us."

The engine sounds grew faint. Hunter couldn't help but believe every second they were forced to wait was another one closer to the SUV finding them.

Down the road, the engine noise grew stronger.

"They are coming back," Hope whispered.

"Let's find a safer place to hide." Hunter eased them over to where a grouping of trees would provide coverage. The car made another pass with the light penetrating the woods.

When it disappeared, Hunter grabbed her hand and headed back to the buggy.

"The car just came by looking for us," Hunter told the shocked people inside. He eased the buggy along through the snow drifts.

"How bad is the wheel?" Abe asked. Hunter glanced over his shoulder at the older man, surprised there didn't appear to be any of the earlier anger in Abe's tone.

"Bad. We may not make it across the road in one piece. Once we're close, we should all get out and walk across to lighten the burden."

"*Jah*, but I have an idea," Abe told him. "It's an old bush fix I've used in the past when I broke a wagon spoke."

He had Hunter's full attention. "What do you have in mind?"

Abe slipped off his coat and undid his suspenders. "If we can wrap these around the damaged spoke, it might help keep it together until we can get it fixed properly."

Hunter slowly smiled. "That just might work." He reined the gelding to a stop. "Conrad, can you help?" He'd need some extra muscle to get the suspenders tight enough. Even though Conrad was injured, he was stronger than Abe.

Abe handed him the suspenders and replaced his coat. "I will show you how to do it."

Before Hunter could object, Abe moved to the hole in the back of the buggy.

Hunter climbed from the buggy and hurried around back to assist Abe down and then Conrad.

The three reached the damaged wheel.

"You will have to wrap it tight." Abe gave instructions.

With Conrad's help, they worked the suspenders around the area and snugged it as tight as they could.

Hunter studied the quick fix. "Do you think we will need to use another suspender?"

Abe shook his head. "*Nay*, that will hold. But we'd better hurry." The older man's warning reminded Hunter of the danger coming after them full-force.

The car's engine noise faded as it moved away. Still, there was always the chance it would make another pass. They didn't have long to cross the road and get out of sight.

The damaged wheel felt somewhat steadier as they dodged trees to reach the road. Hunter got everyone out and grabbed the harness near the gelding's neck. The animal treaded down the steep ditch with the buggy rocking back and forth as it followed. Once they'd cleared the ditch, Hunter felt somewhat relieved.

The horse plodded across the road and into the opposite ditch. "Almost there," he whispered to Hope as everyone got back inside. She forced a smile while he tried to push aside the truth. Reaching the abandoned farm was just the beginning. If they couldn't find a way to fix the wheel, they'd have to keep going with Abe's patch. And on top of that, the back of the buggy was wide open, exposing everyone to the elements. There was still a long way to go before they reached Penny's farm. Had they survived unspeakable odds only to find they were too late to save Penny's life? Too late to save themselves?

TEN

The buggy held together, thanks to her *daed*'s bush fix. She was proud of him for coming up with a way to fix the spoke, though not really surprised. He was always handy. Her *mamm* used to say he could fix anything—no matter how serious—with just his suspenders.

"Conrad, how far before we should be at the house?" Hunter asked again, drawing Hope's thoughts away from better times.

"The drive will be covered and we won't be able to see it. We're close, though." Conrad seemed to have doubts.

With the weather continuing to bear down on them, Hope was worried. If they missed the property by even a little bit in either direction, they might never find it.

And then what?

"Are there any landmarks we can watch for?" Hope asked. She remembered Conrad telling her he'd done some work in the past for several of the *Englischers* on this side.

Conrad shook his head and then stopped. "Wait, there is. There's an old smokehouse at the front of the property. It's sort of close to the road. At least, it was there the last time I worked here."

Hope tried not to give in to the sinking feeling. She'd put her trust in *Gott*. He would see them through. He would protect Penny.

Her feet were frozen despite thick socks and boots, and her hands were numb. She did her best to ignore the discomfort. This trip had been harrowing for everyone. The strain on Naomi and the baby was far greater than anything Hope had gone through, and she was worried. Naomi couldn't lose this baby. Not because some bad men chose to make them part of their deadly games.

"I think I see something." Hunter's excitement grabbed her attention.

Hope squinted through the white visible in front of them and saw what he did. A crumbling smokehouse.

"Thanks be to *Gott*," she murmured with a smile.

Despite their desperate circumstances, Hunter chuckled. "Amen."

He headed the horse toward the smokehouse.

As they drew closer, the remnants of the homestead came into view. A barn stood out bright red. Though faded from years of harsh winters, it was a beacon in the sea of white.

Hunter guided the horse to the barn. "I sure hope there's something inside we can use to fix the wheel."

Hope did, as well, although doubts continued to plague her. This wasn't an Amish farm. The owners probably wouldn't possess any tools for repairing a buggy wheel. She kept her misgivings to herself as Hunter reached the barn.

"I'll get the doors. Can you pull the buggy through?"

Hope stared at the peeling doors on the barn and couldn't let go of her concerns. "*Jah*, I will bring it inside."

She turned his way. Their eyes held. Something shifted in his as they watched each other. She would give anything to know his thoughts.

Hunter blew out a breath, fumbled for the door handle, and opened it. Her heart thundered inside as she watched him open the two swinging doors. One came off its hinges and Hunter almost lost it. Somehow, he managed to hold them open while Hope hurried the horse inside.

Hunter babied the damaged door closed, and pitch black descended immediately. Hope couldn't see anything, and she panicked. Strong arms circled her waist and helped her down. Hunter. They watched each other in the darkness while she struggled to breathe normally. She would give anything to stay with his arms around her, feeling protected. But they needed to repair the wheel and get back on the road. Penny's life was on the line.

Hunter let her go and stepped back. Hope felt her way to the rear of the buggy. While Hunter assisted Conrad, Hope helped Naomi and her father down.

Hope had brought the lantern from the Hilty ranch, though they hadn't been able to use it until now. She retrieved it and struck one of the matches in her pocket to give them light.

With the lantern held high, she and Hunter searched the barn for anything to repair the wheel. The previous owner had removed everything of any value.

"There's nothing useful here." Hunter's disappointment showed on his face. He ran a hand across his eyes. "We have to get it fixed."

"What about the rest of the buildings?" Hope said. "I saw several. And we can search the house. Maybe they left something useful."

He gathered himself and nodded. "You're right. Let's take Conrad with us and see what we can find. To be safe, I'll move the buggy into those woods in case they find the place and check inside the barn."

He and Hope returned to the others.

"There's nothing here to make the repair. Let's hope the rest of the place will hold something useful. Otherwise, we keep going on the damaged wheel."

Once they'd moved the buggy to a safer location, Conrad placed his hands on his *fraa*'s shoulders. "Stay here with Abe. I'll be back."

As soon as they left the protection of the woods, the wind struck hard. Fighting it was next to impossible. She was barely hanging on. Hunter grabbed her arm and looped his through. He was protecting her just like he did when they were together.

"Denki," she said gratefully. Sandwiched between the two men, some of the wind was blocked.

They trudged through the gathered snow until a smaller building emerged through the white. There was a roll-up door that wouldn't budge. Hunter went around to the side and she and Conrad followed. Someone had padlocked the door shut.

"Why would they leave this one locked?" Hope wondered aloud. It didn't make sense. The barn had been cleared out.

"There might be something they want to protect." Hunter made eye contact. "Like a vehicle."

Hope tried not to get too excited. If there was a vehicle locked inside the garage, would it even run?

"We need something to get the doors opened. I'll check the house," Conrad told them.

Hunter stopped him. "We'll go with you. Best to stay together."

After everything they'd been through, staying together and protecting each other was the key to surviving.

"Lead the way," Hunter told Conrad. "You've been here before."

Conrad clutched his coat closer and started for the house.

The distance between the structure and the house felt like forever when her energy was almost gone.

Reaching the run-down house, Conrad tried the back door. It didn't give. "It's locked," he said with a sigh.

"Do the former occupants still come here from time to time?" Hope wasn't acquainted with the family.

Conrad shook his head. "I'm not sure, but I'm guessing we'll find all the other doors locked, as well."

"We'll have to break in." Hunter walked over

to one of the windows. Ice encased the panes of glass. "I wonder if there's anything useful inside. It'll take something big to break the lock on the garage."

The porch was small. Snow had blown in from the side, covering it.

"Let's try around front." Hunter took her hand as if it were a normal thing and she was grateful for the feeling of hers tucked inside his. Together, they stepped off the porch with Conrad. The front of the house was somewhat more protected from the elements.

Hope tried the door, knowing it would be locked. On the far side of the porch, the owners had stacked a couple of big rocks. Maybe after clearing the yard?

"We could use one of these to break the lock." She suggested.

Hunter picked up one of the larger ones and weighed it in his hands. "It might work. This is pretty heavy. Let's take a couple of the others. We might need them."

Hope grabbed one of the rocks while Conrad picked up another. Once they returned to the garage, Hunter positioned the rock above the lock and slammed it hard. It took two more tries before the lock finally broke free.

He dropped the rock. The three put their weight against the door and forced it open.

Inside, the owner had stored a battered Jeep for whatever reason. It was an answer to prayer—if it ran.

"I seem to recall the husband liked to hunt. Maybe he keeps it here for hunting trips." Conrad opened the driver's door. "There's no key."

Had the husband taken the keys with him? It didn't make sense to Hope. What if he accidentally forgot to bring them? He wouldn't be able to use the vehicle. Or maybe the vehicle had been left behind because it didn't run. Why leave the door locked?

"Check around inside." Hunter opened the passenger door. "Hope, look over on that worktable. Maybe he stashed them somewhere out of sight."

She felt around the top of the worktable. Nothing. A set of cabinets had been built above the table.

"They are not in the Jeep," Hunter confirmed as he came over to help her search.

The first cabinet produced a variety of cleaning supplies as well as oil for the Jeep. No keys.

Hope opened the second cabinet and searched. More cleaning supplies. What if they couldn't find the keys?

A tool chest had been shoved beneath the worktable. Hunter opened it. In the bottom of the chest, he pulled out a small metal box.

Hunter twisted the latch free. Two keys on a ring fell out into his hand.

"Those must belong to the Jeep. Let's see if we can get it started." He hurried to the driver's side. Hunter got inside the Jeep and tried the first key. It didn't fit. Taking the second one, he slipped it into the ignition without a problem. His shoulders slumped in relief. He tried to start the vehicle. The Jeep's engine turned over once but didn't fire. A second attempt made a horrible chugging sound followed by clicking.

"The battery is too weak." He glanced down at the gearshift. "It's a manual transmission. We should be able to push start it if it is the battery. Let's get it out of the garage and give it a try."

Conrad opened the roll-up door.

"Hope, can you guide the Jeep out while Conrad and I push? This is going to be different from the car you drove." Hunter explained what she would need to do, then turned the key on. "There's not much fuel in the vehicle. But I see a gas can strapped on back. I hope it's enough to make it to Penny's."

Once he'd put the vehicle in gear, he pointed to a third pedal to the left. "That's the clutch. When I say go, push down on this pedal and turn the wheel. When it starts rolling good, let off on the clutch and give it some gas." He indicated the pedal on the right. "If it is the battery, it should start. Once it does, keep going until you reach the barn, then apply the brake. Hopefully, it will keep running on its own." His brilliant blue eyes searched her face. "Do you understand?"

She swallowed and wished her breathing was steadier. "*Jah*, I understand." But her voice certainly didn't instill confidence.

He held her gaze for a long moment before he stepped back. "*Gut.* Wait for my word."

Hope steadied her hands as Hunter and Conrad moved to the back of the Jeep.

"*Oke*, Hope, step on the clutch."

She pressed with her left foot. "It's down."

Both men started pushing. The vehicle moved forward. Hope grabbed on tight and did her best to keep it from hitting the side of the structure. Once they'd moved past the door, the two men pushed harder.

"Give it some gas," Hunter yelled.

Hope let off the clutch and pressed the gas. The Jeep lurched and sputtered before the engine fired. It was working on its own. She kept her attention on the path ahead while the Jeep traversed the snowy way as if it were nothing. The barn came up fast. Hope slowly edged off on the gas and eased her foot onto the brake.

"Please don't let it die," she whispered, her breath chilling the air in front of her.

The Jeep slowed. She pressed harder until it came to a stop with the engine still running.

Hunter and Conrad caught up with her as Hope opened the door. Hunter leaned past her and put the vehicle in Park. "You handled that as if you've been driving for years." His smile caught her off guard and she couldn't look away.

Hope became aware of Conrad watching their exchange curiously and she climbed from the Jeep.

Hunter cleared his throat and looked away. "We should bring the others out and leave while we still can."

Staying between the two men, Hope opened the door and they entered the barn.

"We found a vehicle," Hope told her *daed* and Naomi. "We can stay warm while we travel." The relief on Naomi's face was worth the struggle of getting the Jeep going.

"Once we reach Mason's house and we're all safe, I'll ride back here and take care of the horse and return the Jeep," Hunter told her father.

Daed nodded his approval before he helped Naomi down.

When everyone was safely inside the warmth of the Jeep, Hunter climbed behind the wheel and put it in gear.

Staring at the never-ending sear of white outside the windshield, Hope's thoughts returned to Penny. "I hope we are not too late," she told Hunter. Since learning Penny was the target of these dangerous men, she couldn't stop worrying. The child was only a few days old. As difficult as it would be to bring the *boppli* out in this weather, it would be worse for Penny and the child if they stayed. Eventually those men would find them.

Up ahead, the adjoining road became visible. Hunter braked slowly and squinted in the direction they'd traveled before. "I don't see anything." His gaze shifted to her. They'd been through so much already. She wasn't sure how many more attacks they could withstand.

Hope covered his hand with hers. "You're doing everything you possibly can."

"I just pray it will be enough." A breath escaped and he eased forward onto the road.

As much as she hoped the rest of the trip would be a peaceful one, the feeling growing stronger through each mile almost assured Hope they had not seen the last of the people chasing them.

She kept her attention on the side mirror. Before today, Hope could not have imagined being caught up in such a situation or being close to Hunter again. Yet if she and Naomi hadn't gone to his home, those men would have eventually killed them both.

"I wonder where they are." Had the SUV gotten back on the road? Where was the car?

A frown marred Hunter's handsome face. "No sign of anyone so far."

"Do you think we missed them while at the house?"

He shook his head. "Under these conditions, it would take them a while to get the tire repaired, if they had a spare. Perhaps the second car went back to assist. Maybe they realized the weather was too much to battle and returned to the community to wait it out?"

After being so determined? She didn't believe it for a minute and doubted Hunter did, either.

"Who was this person they were waiting for?" she asked. "Who else would know how to find Penny, except—"

"Except for her husband," Hunter finished for her. "She told you he wasn't in the picture any longer. Maybe she left him and he wasn't happy about it."

Hope recalled the few conversations she'd had with Penny. Something she'd forgotten about came to mind. "I think there was definitely someone in her life. I remember Penny taking a call once. She went into another room, but I heard her tell the person she loved them."

Hunter's eyes held shock. "If not the husband, then who? A family member?" He shook his head. "We'll never figure it out until Penny explains."

He shifted his attention back to the road. Hope settled in her seat and studied his strong profile. She'd missed spending time with Hunter through the years. Missed the love they'd once shared.

He glanced her way suddenly and caught her watching. Hope jerked toward the side mirror while willing away these heartbreaking thoughts. Their lives had taken different paths and they were all facing danger.

Hope looked over her shoulder. "How are you feeling?" she asked Naomi, hating that her voice wasn't anywhere close to normal. Had Hunter heard?

Naomi leaned heavily against her husband. "Ready for this to be over." But she smiled.

"Me, too. Soon. It will be soon." Hope prayed it would prove true. Because fighting an enemy whose motives were unknown had proved to be an impossible battle so far.

Hunter's hands shook on the wheel. He prayed Hope didn't notice. As much as he wished differently, he could not deny there were feelings in his heart for her still. Despite how things ended between them, he would always care for Hope and wish the best for her.

The Jeep crawled along the road. With the blizzard conditions not letting up and unable to use the headlights, Hunter was terrified he'd drive the vehicle off the road to whatever danger waited there even at this slow speed. The ground beneath them had begun to climb. They were heading for another series of hills before they entered the valley where Penny's home lay.

The Jeep didn't have snow chains and the climb was causing the tires to slip. He stopped in the middle of the road.

"What are you doing?" Hope turned to peer through the frosted back window as if expecting trouble.

"Engaging the Jeep's four-wheel drive capability. We're going to need it going up these hills." Under the best of conditions, the road had several hairpin curves that could prove deadly.

With the four-wheel drive engaged, he continued as his heart drummed at an accelerated pace. Nothing showed behind them. Still…

"You're worried, too," Hope whispered loud enough for only him to hear.

There was no point in denying it. "*Jah.* There are so many things we don't know—like where the SUV and car are now and, more important, why this is happening."

She nodded. "I wish I'd asked Penny more questions. At the time, nothing about her sent up any warnings. Looking back, after what we've gone through, I can see there were many things about her behavior that didn't make sense."

Hunter agreed. "She is obviously running away from something—clearly these men—but the only question is why."

Hope bit her lip. "I can't believe she'd be involved in anything illegal. She's just someone caught up in a situation beyond her control."

She had a gentle heart for those in need. Always had. Hope went out of her way to help the hurting. He'd always admired that about her.

The Jeep sputtered a couple of times, jerking his attention back to the gauges.

"What's wrong?" Her worried face latched onto him.

The fuel gage had slipped even lower. "We are running low on gas. I hope the fuel can strapped to the back has enough to get us there."

"We have a long way to go still. We'll never make it through the hills on foot."

She was right. They could die up here from exposure.

Though he didn't understand a whole lot about modern vehicles, he knew enough to realize how much trouble they'd be in if they ran out of fuel. "I'm going to stop and try to refuel."

Both he and Hope climbed out and went around to the back where the can was bungee tied to the spare tire.

Hunter unfastened the can and lifted it free. Relief flew through his body when he shook it. "It's more than half full. That should get us to Mason's if the gas isn't too old and is usable."

Hunter removed the gas cap and poured in the fuel. "It doesn't look as if it's gone bad." While he worked, he kept a careful watch on the road behind them. Once the can was empty, he and Hope returned to the vehicle.

On a whim, Hunter pulled out one of the cell phones and tried the sheriff with the same response. He didn't use phones other than the occasional necessary call at the phone shanty. Though Mason had showed him the satellite phone he used as part of the county's search and rescue team, Hunter couldn't recall the number off the top of his head.

"Hunter, I see something." Conrad's troubled voice whipped Hunter's attention behind them. Through the thick snowfall, bits of light shone. His heart sank. After fighting so hard, they were no closer to being safe than when Hope had first showed up at his home.

"We need to get off this road now." Hunter looked for a safe place to exit. After what happened before with Hope almost falling to her death, he knew the dangers hidden in the hills.

Hope leaned forward. "I don't see anything... wait—over there." She pointed. "If we can get the Jeep into those trees, we should be out of reach of the headlights."

Hunter steered the Jeep over the snow-covered ditch and up the other side into the woods. The only lights visible were from the dash. If the men glanced this way, would they see the lights? He removed his coat and laid it over the dash to hide them.

The silence was filled with his panicked breaths and those of the others. The headlights from the vehicle illuminated the road.

Hope reached for his hand. Holding hers felt as natural as drawing his next breath.

No one said a word as the lights grew stronger. The vehicle crawled along the road.

Glimpses through the trees revealed a large vehicle. The SUV.

A terrifying thought occurred. Where was the car?

The SUV eventually passed. Soon the lights were gone, as well.

"Where's the second vehicle?" He shifted to Hope and searched her face.

"Maybe they left it and decided to take just the one."

Possibly, and yet he couldn't let down his guard. "Let's give it a little time before we get back on the road."

The heater kept it comfortable inside. Still, they couldn't afford to stay here for long. The fuel would not last forever and every second Penny and the baby were at her house alone they were in danger.

But where was the car? The question drummed in his head.

After a long amount of time passed, Hunter grabbed his coat and slipped it on. He eased the Jeep back toward the road. At the edge of the trees, he leaned forward and squinted through the icy window. Nothing appeared through the battering storm.

Protect us...

The prayer slipped through his head as Hunter guided the Jeep onto the road. While they didn't know where the car had gone, with the SUV in front, it could prove a deadly threat if they were caught in between the two.

His knuckles turned white from squeezing the wheel. Worry came from all directions. The vehicles. Penny. The truth behind what was happening.

Using the headlights wasn't an option. Their only choice? Keep creeping along through this dangerous countryside.

Hunter eased around another hairpin curve and breathed a sigh of relief. He relaxed a little. They were okay.

Something in the rearview mirror looked out of place. Gone too quick to say for sure. Was he being paranoid?

He returned his attention to the road ahead. It had enough dangers of its own. They were coming into another deadly curve.

Hunter leaned forward, strangling the wheel in his hands.

"What is that?"

Hunter didn't have time to untangle the meaning of Hope's question before something slammed against the back of the Jeep hard, sending them jolting forward. He swung around in time to see bright lights replace the whiteout. The car. Right on their bumper.

One false move and they would go careering over the side of the hill to an uncertain future.

The car didn't waste time slamming into them again. The Jeep swerved from the momentum, shifting closer to the edge of the road.

Hope shrieked and gripped the door. Naomi moaned.

Not like this. He couldn't let it end like this. Hunter fought the wheel with all he had and somehow managed to keep it on the road. But for how long?

Once more, the bright lights were right on top of them, ready to attack. Hunter dodged to the left—almost hit the solid rock of the hillside—then swerved back onto the road. The car sped up, positioned for another blow.

Hunter yanked the wheel once more. The car caught the Jeep with a glancing blow to the back left corner. While he struggled to control their momentum, he hit a patch of black ice beneath the snow and spun three hundred and sixty degrees, striking the car hard on the driver's side.

The man behind the wheel was close enough for Hunter to see his determination shift to fear as the car quickly veered to the right despite his efforts to change directions.

"They're going over!" Abe exclaimed, a look of horror on his face.

"I can't believe it." Hope watched the car careering from the road. It flew off the side, hung in air, suspended for a moment in time, then dropped from their view.

Hunter stopped the Jeep and bailed out along with the others. They rushed to the edge of the road. The car hit the surface below with a loud bang. It burst into flames almost immediately.

None of the men inside the car would have survived the fall much less the fire. That could just as easily have been them.

Flames licked up from the wreckage. Hunter's hands shook as his mind relived what they'd gone through.

How long before the men in the SUV spotted the fire? "We have to get out of here," he told the group. "The other vehicle is still out there somewhere." The occupants of the car might have called their partners before they'd lost control.

Reaching the Jeep, Hunter inspected the limited damage. It had a scratch on the bumper and a large dent where it had struck the car. Nothing to prevent them from continuing.

Once inside, Hunter tried to control his shaking hands enough to guide the Jeep around another winding upward curve. More than ever, he wished they could use the headlights, but after what happened, he didn't trust they wouldn't be found out.

It felt like it took forever to climb the hill. Once they'd crested, Hunter prepared for the harrowing trip downhill. He shifted into the lowest gear possible and let off the brake pedal.

Hope fixed eyes full of worry on him.

He realized she was picking up all his anxieties and he tried to change that. "We will be *oke*."

She slowly nodded and faced the windshield.

Hunter kept a tight hold on the wheel and his attention on the road as the Jeep picked up speed even in the low gear. He did his best to stay off the brakes. The last thing they needed was for something else to go wrong.

With visibility a minimum of a few feet in front of the hood, his shoulders ached from tension and being hunched over the wheel.

"Hunter." Hope grabbed his arm suddenly.

She pointed to something down the hill. The SUV. They were in real trouble.

ELEVEN

Hope looked for a safe place to hide, but there was no guarantee they wouldn't meet the same fate as the car if not careful.

"Is there a place coming up to get off the road without plummeting to our deaths?" she asked. Conrad had traveled the mountain passes many times while working at the different homes on this side.

"The landscape levels off a little farther down," Conrad told them.

Hope kept her attention on the advancing SUV. It would be close. She prayed they could get off the road before the headlights homed in on them.

Her heart beat a mile a minute as Hunter picked up the Jeep's speed. She clung to the door as they flew down the road at a frightening pace.

"Almost there," Hunter murmured to himself. The SUV's headlights had disappeared around a curve.

The speed they traveled was scary enough on its own. With the enemy advancing, Hope prayed earnestly for their safety.

The SUV emerged from behind the curve. Another bend and then it would be heading straight for them.

Hurry, Hunter. She couldn't say the words out loud. Hunter was doing everything in his power to save them. Their lives were in *Gott*'s hands now.

Hope kept her attention on the curve where the SUV had disappeared. The Jeep reached safer ground and Hunter slowed the speed enough to leave the road.

The headlights reappeared. The SUV was entering the straight stretch. The Jeep rocked back and forth precariously through the rough terrain while Hope couldn't take her eyes off the SUV. It was heading straight for them.

The Jeep cleared the ditch and headed for the trees along the road. Seconds later, the SUV passed by.

Hope blew out a breath and clutched Hunter's arm. "That was much too close."

The stress of what he'd gone through showed on Hunter's tight expression. "I don't know how many more of those we can survive."

His words sent alarming tremors through her body. They'd cheated death many times already on this desperate trek. They were all weary and barely hanging on. How many more run-ins would they be able to walk away from?

Hunter's breathing matched hers. Hope glanced back at the people she loved. "How are you all holding up?"

Three sets of worried expressions glued to hers. Answer enough.

"You did a *gut* job back there." Her *daed* directed the rare compliment Hunter's way.

Hunter couldn't believe the high praise from Abe. *"Denki,"* he muttered. "It's not safe to use the road again." Hunter retrieved one of the cell phones from his pocket and prepared to try the sheriff again. He stopped with the phone still in his hand. "Mason told me there is a way to track a cell phone." He shot her a look. "What if they are tracking us?"

Was that how the men kept finding them? Hunter had left the phone on after his last attempt.

Hunter tried to make a call again with the same results. He quickly turned the phone off. "Mason said if it's off, it is harder to track." He shoved the device back into his coat pocket.

Hope's heart rate wouldn't slow. She studied the snowy woods. From what she could see, they were on level ground. "Can we make it this way?"

Hunter shook his head. "I'm not sure. Conrad, am I missing anything or is there a lot of pastureland coming up?"

Conrad nodded. "You're right. There are several open fields straight ahead."

Hunter started forward through the trees.

How long before the men in the SUV realized they had escaped?

The Jeep plowed through the deep snow while Hunter kept his attention on the uneven territory cluttered with fallen tree branches and stubs that rocked the vehicle so much Hope became more concerned for Naomi's welfare. She looked back at her friend. "Do we need to stop?"

"Could we please?"

Hunter brought the Jeep to a quick halt. Hope turned in her seat to study the pregnant woman. "What are you feeling?"

Naomi didn't answer for a long time. "I'm uncomfortable. The rocking makes me feel sick."

They couldn't keep going like this.

"Tell me when you're feeling better." Hope did what she could to make her patient more comfortable. "Are you experiencing any pain?"

Naomi shook her head. "*Nay.* Just the nausea. It will pass."

Hope searched Naomi's face before she slowly shifted forward. "I'm worried," she whispered for only Hunter. "This has all been too much for her."

"We will let her rest for a little while longer. Once we get Penny and the baby, we'll head for Mason's. She can lie down there."

She blew out a breath and pushed back her loose hair from her face before turning to him. "*Denki*, Hunter, for everything you're doing." Looking into his blue eyes made her heart ache anew for the things they'd once wanted.

He touched her cheek. "I'm sorry," he murmured. "Sorry for my part in destroying our future."

Her heart broke. She fought back tears. "It was not your fault." She was just as much to blame. Hope turned away. With so many listening, now was not the time for this discussion.

"I'm feeling better now," Naomi murmured, drawing Hope's attention to her. She attempted a smile for her friend.

Hunter slowly started through the woods without looking at Hope again. She did her best to bury the hurt once more.

The Jeep jostled over the uneven terrain. Hope could see the road to their left through the trees. If the occupants of the SUV couldn't tell which vehicle went over the side of the mountain, they'd have to investigate to be sure. It would buy them some time. Hopefully, it would be enough to reach Penny's home.

Hunter's full attention was on his driving. Guilt made her say, "I'm sorry, too."

He turned slightly but it was enough to see the pain on his face that broke her heart. They'd both hurt each other badly.

"It is *oke*," he murmured in a strained tone.

It was something. They hadn't spoken a single word to each other in years. Perhaps there was a chance to reclaim something of the friendship they'd once shared.

"We should be far enough away that it will be safe to take the road again." Hunter eased the Jeep onto the road and was faced with another sweeping curve. Hope thought about her *mamm*. Her mother had put her faith above everything. Family and friends were an important second. Hope often wondered what her mother might say if she'd lived to see the argument between her husband and Levi. The two men had been friends since they were toddlers. They'd briefly worked together before her father went out on his own and created his logging company.

Though her *daed* pretended to hold on to his anger toward Levi, there were times when she'd seen him looking out the window with an expression that tore at her heart. She believed having his dear friend die before he could re-

pair the damage was one of his biggest regrets.
Maybe it was time to change the course of her
and Hunter's future before it was too late so
they didn't end up living in regret over what
might have been.

I'm sorry, too. Her words struck like a knife
to his heart. Instead of feeling relief he and
Hope might finally be patching up their friendship, he believed it marked the end of the dream
he harbored in his heart of one day being re-
united with her.

He was sorry. So sorry for letting something
tear them apart. They'd both been so foolish
back then. So determined each of their fathers
was right. Willing to give up everything to
stand behind something that didn't matter.

His jaw flexed. Where did he and Hope go
from here? Back to being friends? Why did the
thought of friendship hurt so much? Maybe because, as hard as he tried to see a happy ending
for them, he didn't.

He struggled to let the hurt go. Surviving
what they were going through had to be the
most important thing on his mind right now.
He'd deal with the rest once this ended.

"Are we getting closer?" Hunter asked the
woman responsible for the ache in his heart.

Hope leaned forward and studied the layout near the road while he struggled. Some chances only came around once in a lifetime. He'd learned to be happy without her in his life. Why was he insisting on dredging up old hurts now?

"Maybe a few more miles." He barely heard what she said. Hunter sat straighter and fought against feelings of hopelessness when the truth became clear.

"*Gut*, because I see headlights close to where the car went off the road," he said, low for only her to hear. "Don't look behind us," he urged when she would have. "No need to worry the others. The lights do not appear to be moving. Yet."

The terror on her face was hard to see.

"Don't give up," he whispered and claimed her hand once more.

Hope bit back a sob and turned away.

Her reaction surprised him. Was she exhausted from what they'd been through? Or was something more responsible for her reaction?

Hunter fixed his gaze on the rearview mirror. The SUV was on the move again.

Hope glanced in the side mirror. "We are almost to Penny's turnoff. We have to make it."

There was no other choice. If they didn't reach the cutoff before the SUV found them…

Tension consumed his body.

"I don't think we can risk using the road again, but going across the rough countryside was difficult on Naomi before." Hunter looked over his shoulder to where Naomi rested her head on Conrad's shoulder. "I don't know what to do."

Hope's expression softened with compassion. "Let's worry about getting Penny and her *sohn*. *Gott* will show us the right path from there."

Hunter wanted to believe it, but holding on to that promise was hard after everything they'd been through. He kept a close watch on the mirror. The SUV was traveling quickly. Had they realized the vehicle at the bottom of the hill wasn't the Jeep?

"Where is the turnoff?" He couldn't see anything.

Hope leaned in close to the windshield. "I only visited Penny a few times, but the turnoff is overgrown and hard to find."

What if they missed it in the storm?

"We're close," she assured him. "There are a couple of large trees before we reach it. They look like one big tree, but I realized they are actually two growing close together. There! Those are the trees." He saw them. "The drive is past them."

Hunter slowed enough to prepare to turn.

A quick look confirmed the SUV was getting closer.

"Hurry, Hunter," Hope whispered and grabbed the door when he braked too hard after nearly missing the path.

"Sorry," he murmured as he turned from the road. The drive was almost as bad as the wilderness they'd traveled through.

"What if they follow us?" The terror in her voice was unmistakable. If the SUV was able to pick up which way they'd gone, they'd be leading the men straight to Penny.

"We don't have a choice." He prayed the conditions would work in their favor.

As he urged the Jeep down the overgrown path, his heart wouldn't slow to normal. His faith had taught him everything that happened was at *Gott*'s will, yet for the life of him, Hunter couldn't understand how what they were going through could be part of *Gott*'s *gut* plan. Why would He wish for a mother to be hunted down by these dangerous men, putting so many lives in danger? How could what happened between him and Hope be in *Gott*'s will?

"There are lights out on the road," Abe said, interrupting Hunter's angry thoughts.

Hunter turned in time to see glimpses of headlights through the trees. Through the exhaustion, he tried to think. Even if the SUV's occupants didn't see their tracks, there was always the risk of running into their pursuers after they had Penny and her son.

His worst nightmare was they'd end up dead and no one would ever know why these dangerous men chose to harm so many. He couldn't let that happen. No matter what, he had to keep fighting to save their lives.

If they were forced to continue cross-country to Mason's, there were fences to be dealt with. He'd have to find something to cut the wire and allow them to pass through. Perhaps Penny would have wire cutters or something else that might work.

The headlights faded from view. Hunter blew out a relieved sigh when nothing but the storm appeared behind them.

"I think they've kept going," he said with a sigh of relief. "Let's do this quickly. Hope, while you help Penny prepare for the trip, I'll see if I can find something to cut the fence. We'll have to be quick about it." It sounded easy enough. Get Penny—go on their way. Yet nothing about this trip had been easy.

With his mind foggy from the unimaginable things they'd survived, stringing together a coherent thought seemed impossible.

Help me, Gott. He had to keep his wits about

him. People were counting on him. Hope was counting on him.

He released the brake and eased down the drive. Almost finished. This was almost over.

Nothing about the property was familiar. Though he'd passed by this place many times—even recently—Hunter had always assumed it remained vacant. He'd never ventured down the drive. Had no idea what was waiting for them at the house.

A gut-wrenching thought occurred. What if the men had already been to the house? There could be people waiting for them, or worse, he and the other weary souls with him might find Penny deceased.

The Jeep bounced over the collection of holes in the drive. The snow coverage prevented Hunter from seeing them. Some were deep enough to do damage to a normal vehicle. Thankfully, the Jeep was off-road capable. Still, he regretted every single one he struck because he'd seen Naomi's pained expression in the mirror.

The drive wound its way through trees and overgrown scrub brush while Hunter kept a close watch in the rearview mirror, terrified the SUV would appear behind them in a blink of the eye. If that happened, they would be trapped here with no way to escape.

"We are almost to the house," Hope assured him as if she'd seen his fears.

Hunter's gut twisted with anxiety. The blusterous wind slapped snow at the windshield faster than the wipers could keep up. Without the lights, it was next to impossible to see anything. The tension created by the storm and the men following them pressed down on him like a heavy weight. He'd been through some situations before when he'd helped his *bruder* Aaron and his wife Victoria when she was being hunted by bad people. He'd witnessed firsthand the effects dangerous people bent on trouble had on his family and the community. Yet Hunter never thought he'd find himself caught up in a situation like this.

"There it is!" Hope exclaimed when he cleared the tree coverage and encountered the full force of the storm.

Hunter spotted the house. He kept going until they were almost right on top of it, then shoved the gear into Park. Not a single light shone through the curtains.

It's the middle of the night, his head told him. It stood to reason Penny would be sleeping.

Still, what if the darkness was due to something more? What if Penny was gone or men waited inside? They could be walking into an ambush.

Hunter faced those in the back seat. "Stay here. Let Hope and me make contact first, just in case." As much as he didn't want to involve Hope, she knew the young mother. If Penny had any inkling of why these men were after her, she might be too afraid to open the door.

He turned to Hope with regret. "I'm sorry. I wish I didn't have to involve you."

Before he even finished, she shook her head. "No, Hunter, I have to go. Penny will recognize my voice." She stared up at the house, a shiver playing through her frame.

He held her gaze. There were so many things he wanted to say, but he couldn't. "Are you ready?"

She stared into his eyes for the longest time before finally nodding.

"Conrad, keep watch. If you see the SUV, get everyone inside the house."

Conrad agreed.

Together Hunter and Hope left the Jeep and hurried up to the porch.

"I really hate bringing such horrible things to her," Hope said before she knocked several times and waited. Nothing stirred inside. "She's probably still sleeping."

Hunter wanted that to be the case. "We don't have a choice. We have to wake her." This was no time for polite behavior. When Hope's knocks didn't garner a response, Hunter leaned past her and pounded as loudly as he could.

He listened carefully. It was hard to hear anything above the storm. If he had to, he'd break down the door.

"She may be too afraid to open the door," he told her. "Why don't you let her know it's you?"

"Penny, it's Hope Christner. Open the door. This is an emergency."

The porch light switched on. A young *Englischer* woman peeked out the curtained window in the door. The first impression to strike Hunter was that she looked scared to death. As if she were expecting trouble.

Penny spotted Hope and quickly unlocked the door. She pulled it open, her troubled eyes skirting past Hope to Hunter.

"Why are you here? What's happened?" Her face was pale in the porch light, and her dark hair was tied back in a ponytail.

"Something has happened. Men came to my house looking for you." Hope glanced back at the people in the Jeep. "And they could be close now. I'm sorry, Penny, I know it's late, but we have to leave. Now."

Penny's shocked eyes grew large. She clasped her hand over her mouth. "They're here. How did they find me?"

"I believe they have someone who knows

where you're staying. Go inside. I'll get the others and bring them in until we're ready to leave."

Penny snapped out of her fear. "I'm sorry. Please, come inside and warm yourselves. You must be frozen. I'll get the baby ready."

Hunter stopped Hope before she went inside. "I'm going to move the Jeep around back, just in case."

She understood what he meant. "Be careful, Hunter."

"I will." He memorized every inch of her pretty face. If they survived this, would there be the chance for them to clear the air? To find their way back to each other? He wanted that so desperately. "Go inside with her. I'll be right back."

Hope went with Penny while Hunter returned to the Jeep. "Take the others inside to warm up," he told Conrad after his friend hopped out and he explained about moving the Jeep. Like it or not, with the Jeep's weak battery, they'd have to leave it running or they might not be able to start it again.

Hunter helped Abe from the back, followed by Naomi. "I'll meet you inside in a few minutes."

Conrad placed his arm around Naomi. The three headed up the steps and went inside.

Hunter glanced down the path they'd traveled. They'd be on their way in no time. Soon, all of this would be a bad memory. So why didn't he feel a sense of relief?

Hunter climbed behind the wheel. Pulling the Jeep around without the lights was every bit as difficult as the last miles they'd traveled without them. The property hadn't been cleared in years and there were lots of dangers. He was grateful when he finished the task.

Hunter traversed the thick accumulation to the front of the house once more. He listened intently. The SUV had probably kept going. Still, Hunter walked some ways down the drive. No sign of headlights. No sound of the powerful engine.

As much as he wanted to believe they were going to be okay, the knot twisting inside his stomach wouldn't let him. Hunter noticed a small garage detached from the house. He went inside. To get through the fences standing between the properties, he'd need wire cutters or something equally strong. A small vehicle was parked inside, and a workbench sat against one wall. Hunter dug around and found a set of pliers that would have to work on the fence. He stuck them in his pocket.

With nothing but the storm as a current danger, Hunter climbed the steps to the porch and went inside.

Hope stood beside Penny and an infant. Her fearful eyes gripped his.

"So far, no one is coming this way," he told her.

Her shoulders visibly relaxed. "Oh, thank You, *Gott*."

"Do you know who these men are?" Hunter asked Penny. After everything they'd been through, he had to know why. And he believed she could answer the question.

Penny's eyes filled with tears. "Yes, I know. He's a bad man who doesn't care who he hurts to get what he wants. I just can't believe he found me. I was so sure I'd be safe here."

Hunter forgot all about the urgency to leave. "What do you mean?" he asked the young woman. "Has he done something to you before?"

When Penny didn't speak, Hope asked, "Is this man your husband?"

Penny struggled to speak for the longest time. "No, he isn't my husband." Her voice died into a sob. "He killed my husband."

Hunter couldn't believe he'd heard correctly. "Who is this man and why would he kill your husband? Why is he coming after you? What is this really about?"

Penny glanced down at the child in her arms. "Money," she said softly. "It's about money." The baby cooed softly and she smiled through her tears. "He is my husband's cousin, Stephen Jackson. He called me earlier and told me he'd killed my husband, Frank, and my baby and I were next if I didn't tell him where we were hiding. I was so scared. I didn't know what to do."

"Start by telling us what's going on. Let us help you," Hunter beseeched her.

Penny wiped her palm across her eyes. "Stephen and several of the men he hangs out with robbed a bank in Billings several weeks back."

This was bad—truly bad. He had a really dreadful feeling the worst was yet to come. Hunter went over to the window and looked out. No sign of this Jackson man or the others. But if they did have someone who could tell them where Penny was hiding, it would only be a matter of time before they found the house—storm or not.

TWELVE

The man who had threatened them had killed Penny's husband. Hope couldn't imagine the terror Penny had gone through at this man's hands.

"Stephen showed up at our house in Eagle's Nest after the robbery. He said him and his buddies needed to hide out for a while." Penny visibly shivered. "To tell you the truth, he gave me the creeps, and his friends were no better. I'd never met Stephen before then."

She absently rocked the *boppli* in her arms. Hope wondered if she was even aware of doing so.

"Stephen and the others would watch the news all the time. When it mentioned the bank robbery in Billings, they were practically glued to the TV. You see, Stephen lived in Billings and he'd been in and out of trouble for years, according to Frank. I should have known he was the one who'd robbed the bank. Stephen and the others were constantly watching out the windows as if they expected someone to show up at the door at any time."

"The police," Hope said. "They were looking for the police."

Penny nodded. "Yes, exactly. My husband and I figured out soon enough they had robbed the bank. Frank asked them to leave. Stephen became furious. I thought he would kill Frank right then, but he just told Frank they'd go, but he was leaving something there for safe keeping. He'd come back and get it when the attention was off the robbery."

Out of the corner of her eye, Hope noticed Hunter's continuous attention out the window.

"Did they leave?" Hope prompted.

Penny nodded. "Yes, but they left a duffel bag in the basement and they told Frank and me if we told anyone about them being there, or about the bag, they'd kill us."

Hunter stepped from the window. "As much as I want to hear the rest of this, we really have to go. It's too dangerous to stay here any longer. Gather what you need for the child and we'll head out."

Hope went with her to help.

"I can't believe this is happening," Penny said, running a nervous hand across her forehead, her attention on her precious *sohn*.

"We're going to Hunter's brother's home, where we'll be safe." Hope told her about trying to call the sheriff's station without any results. "Mason was once in law enforcement. He will know what to do."

Penny put as many things as she could fit into her diaper bag while holding her child close. "I'm ready." She handed Hope the bag. Together they returned to the living room.

Hunter immediately pulled her aside. "We have a problem."

Hope's heart sank. How much more could they take? "What is it?"

"The Jeep is leaking fuel. I went outside to check it before we left. I used the flashlight since I'd parked around back. There was a pool of liquid beneath. Gas. There's no way we can make it to Mason's like this."

The news threatened to break her. "What do we do?"

He glanced past her to Penny. "There's a vehicle in the garage. We'll have to use it. I don't think there's time to drain the fuel from your vehicle and place it in the Jeep, even if we had the ability."

With the leaking fuel tank they'd risk running out of fuel along the way, not to mention leaving a trail behind that would be easy to follow.

Penny didn't hesitate. "Of course we can take

it. The keys are right here." She went over to the kitchen counter. Rummaging through a drawer, she brought out a set of keys. "I keep it out of sight because, well, you can guess."

Hunter accepted them from her and turned to Hope. "I'll get it. It will be best to keep the *boppli* and the others out of the weather as much as possible." Hunter started for the front of the house.

"I'm coming with you." They'd been through so much together. She wouldn't let him do this alone. Something akin to admiration flashed in his eyes before he nodded.

"Be careful, *dochder*," her father warned before the two stepped out into the blizzard.

Hope's stomach twisted as she followed Hunter from the porch. Her body felt as if it were permanently numbed from the cold. Her mind, the same. She expected their hunters to show up at any time.

"When will this end?" she asked and wished that there was a clear answer. "It seems at every turn—just when we think we're finally out of trouble—something else happens. Like the Jeep's fuel tank being damaged." It was too much.

Hunter tugged her into the protection of his arms. "Don't give up, Hope. We are close. As soon as we get to Mason's, we can breathe again."

Until then, a whole lot of uncertainties stood between them and safety.

Hunter opened the garage door and held it for her. Hope stepped inside. He followed and closed it behind them. "There are lights." Hunter flipped on the overhead light. The small sedan Penny had driven to her house was tucked inside. "It will be a tight fit for all of us, but we don't have a choice. At least it has four-wheel drive, so we should be able to go off road without too much of a problem."

The weariness on his handsome face was testament to how hard he'd fought for them all.

Hope couldn't help herself. She touched his cheek. "No matter what happens, none of us would be alive if it weren't for you." She fought back tears. They might not survive this, and she wanted to be clear. "I'm so sorry for what happened between us, Hunter. I've wished a thousand times that I could change the outcome."

Hunter closed his eyes and covered her hand with his. "I'm the one who is sorry. I put other things—family loyalties—ahead of you, and it wasn't right. I should have told you how much you meant to me. I should have stood by you."

Tears fell from her eyes. She hugged him close. While there could be no rewriting the past, if they didn't make it out of this, she couldn't think of anyone else she would want to be at her side through the end.

Sometimes, it takes almost losing everything to realize what you'd given up. He knew that now. Was it too late for them to fix the damage they'd done to their relationship?

The hopeless look in her eyes was a knife to his heart. Hunter clasped her hand in his and brought it to his lips. He kissed her knuckles and then let her go.

He would fight for her—battle every corrupt man out there to keep her alive. No matter what happened to him, even if it cost him his life, he'd fight for her.

"We should get the others and leave while we still can. If these men are motivated by money, they won't stop until they have it." He looked deep into her eyes. Memorized every detail of her pretty face. Wished more than ever he could take all the pain away.

It broke his heart when she turned away because it felt like she was rejecting him once more. Would they ever be able to repair the past or did the hurt cut too deep?

He held open the passenger door and Hope climbed in, then he raised the overhead garage door before getting behind the wheel.

Hunter started the vehicle and put it in gear. He drove to the front of the house.

Once he'd stopped, he looked over at her, wishing there was something he could do to make what they faced easier. But there wasn't. "We'd better go."

He left the vehicle running and got out with Hope to enter the house.

"Is everyone ready?" The weary faces of those who had been right there with them through every dangerous move looked to him to get them safely to Mason's home.

Every second they sat idle, the likelihood of those men finding them increased.

"Let's get Penny and the *boppli* situated in the back and then Naomi." Hunter grabbed the diaper bag and headed for the door. "Quickly, Penny." The young mother nodded and followed him to the door. With her and Naomi close, he pulled in a breath and stepped out onto the porch.

"Follow me." With the child swaddled against Penny's body for additional warmth, she stepped outside. Hunter clasped her arm to protect her from the slippery steps and moved to the edge of the porch with Naomi close, her husband holding her hand.

Hope and Abe followed. Hunter squinted through the dark, cold night, but he couldn't see anything through the blizzard. He started down the steps with Penny and had almost reached the vehicle when he glanced over his shoulder to where Hope stood on the porch. She wasn't moving.

"Hurry, Hope." He couldn't understand why she wasn't coming with them. Following her gaze, he saw that she wasn't looking at him but at something past his shoulder. Hunter spun on his heel and his heart plummeted. Through the trees a glimpse of light—headlights.

They were too late.

"Get everyone back inside," Hunter told her. He assisted Penny to the porch where Conrad helped her and his wife inside. If he could get the vehicle into the garage, those men might not check the structure and realize the vehicle had been running recently. Maybe they'd think the place was abandoned...unless they had inside knowledge that the property belonged to Penny's family.

Hope ushered her father inside and closed the door before returning to Hunter. "Whatever you have planned, I'm going to help."

"No, Hope." He just wanted to keep her safe.

She didn't listen but opened the passenger door and got inside. He had no choice. It wouldn't be long before the SUV reached them.

Hunter turned the vehicle around and pulled it inside the garage.

"Let's get back to the house," he told her once he'd killed the engine. With her hand tucked in his, they slipped through the side entrance and out into the dark.

Hunter skirted around to the front of the garage. So far, the SUV hadn't reached the house. As soon as they cleared the front, Hunter saw the SUV had reached the bend before the house. Headlights flashed across the countryside. He grabbed Hope and tucked her in behind the protection of the garage. They'd never make it like this.

"Through the trees. We can circle around behind the house." Hunter kept hold of her hand as he tugged her along with him to the woods near the rear of the garage.

His breath was labored from fear as they started through the trees. Reaching the house was just the beginning. How could they possibly hope to fight off so many should it come to that?

Once he and Hope were parallel to the back of the house, they ran to the porch. He knocked several times then tugged Hope close.

Conrad opened the door. "Are they here?"

"Almost." He and Hope crossed the threshold.

Penny hadn't turned on any lights, which would work in their favor.

"Let's make sure all the windows and doors are locked and the curtains are closed." Together with Hope and Conrad, he secured the openings and closed window coverings.

The curtains in front of the house were made of heavy material. Hunter believed they would block the view of anyone standing on the porch.

"Get everyone away from the front." Anything with an outside wall could be dangerous.

"The hallway," Penny told him, and everyone moved there.

"Do you own a weapon?"

Penny shook her head, her eyes large and fearful at the prospect of having to use a weapon.

That meant they had the shotgun and the two weapons they'd taken. Those wouldn't last long against so many.

"What about knives?" Whatever they could use as a deterrent.

"Yes, in the kitchen." Penny started for the room but he stopped her.

"I'll get them." Hunter stepped out into the open with an eerie feeling following him to the kitchen. He found several kitchen knives and brought them back. He had his pocketknife. At least it was something.

"I just remembered my grandfather used to

have a rifle. I think it's still in the closet." Penny pointed to the hall closet.

Hunter looked past the old jackets and shoes and found the rifle leaning against the back wall. It wasn't loaded. He searched around on the top shelf until he located a box of shells gathering dust. Hunter quickly loaded the weapon. As he crossed to the others, nothing showed through the thick curtains. Had the SUV reached the house? If so, would they try to break inside?

He kept remembering what his family had said about tracking cell phones.

"Is your phone turned on?" he asked Penny.

The young mother pulled out the phone from her jeans' pocket. "Do you need to use it?"

Hunter took it from her. "I'm turning it off just to be safe."

Penny lost all color. "I had no idea. I spoke to Stephen on the phone. He called from Frank's phone. He has my number."

Hunter thought about what he and Hope had overheard. "We believe they have someone with them who knows where you are. Do you have any idea who this might be?"

Penny frowned before shaking her head. "Only my husband," she sobbed.

Hope put her arm around Penny. "I'm so sorry."

Penny wept against her side.

"Here, let me take the *boppli*."

Penny handed Hope the child while she struggled to compose herself. She covered her eyes with her hands and wept. "Wait," she said suddenly and looked up, her face ravaged by tears. "There's my grandmother. This was once her home. If they have her..."

The idea of these men using Penny's grandmother against her would have been unimaginable before tonight. They'd threatened a pregnant woman and beat up an old man. They would stop at nothing to get the money they stole.

"You said your husband's cousin agreed to leave. You came here alone? Why didn't your husband come with you?" If the cousin was threatening them both, Hunter didn't understand why he had sent his wife here alone.

"Frank wanted to get me and our child out of harm's way until he could figure how to get us free of his cousin's threat." Her voice broke again.

"He was going to the police," Hunter stated. "Does your grandmother live with you?" Penny hadn't mentioned her grandmother before, so he had doubts.

She shook her head. "No. She has a small house at the edge of Eagle's Nest. She moved there to be closer to us and her doctors when her health began to decline. Granny gave us the farm here, but we couldn't leave her. She needs us." Tears filled Penny's eyes and she brushed them away. "Frank's never even been here before."

"Did your husband tell your cousin about this place?" How else would they know to look in the West Kootenai area for Penny?

"Frank had mentioned it—before he realized how bad Stephen really was—but we never told him the address and he doesn't know what my grandmother's last name is or where she lives even."

Hunter considered what she'd said. How hard would it be for them to find the grandmother's name?

"Frank told me his cousin joked about killing someone before, but Frank thought he'd made it up." Penny shivered. Hunter certainly believed it was true. They'd all witnessed firsthand how ruthless this Jackson fella and his people were.

"Did the police ever question the cousin concerning the robbery? You said he lived in Billings and he had been in trouble before," Hunter asked.

A look of disgust flashed across Penny's face. "Stephen said the police suspected him and his friends. Of course, Stephen denied robbing the bank." Penny gathered in a breath.

"So your husband stayed behind to protect you and the baby," Hunter returned.

She nodded. "Yes. Frank believed Stephen would come back to the house because he had no place else to go and he'd left the money there. Frank told me he was worried Stephen would decide we were a liability and he'd eventually kill us. He sent me here with the money and planned to use it as leverage to get Stephen to leave us alone. He planned to get Stephen to confess to the robbery and secretly record it. Then he'd go to the police with the recording. He asked me to wait for him here with the money until he got the police to arrest Stephen and his crew." She stopped, her bottom lip quivering.

Frank's suspicions came true and Stephen ended up taking her husband's life.

"Stephen called me and told me he only wanted the money. Once he had it, he'd leave me and the baby alone." She scanned the faces gathered around her. "I know he's lying. He'll kill me once he gets it."

Hunter had no doubt. "We can't let that happen." If Jackson had killed before, he wouldn't think twice about taking all their lives once he had the money. "I'm going to try to get a look outside. If they aren't certain this is the place where you're hiding, I'm hoping they'll eventually leave." But what those men had said earlier kept playing through his head. They claimed to have someone who could lead them here. They probably hadn't happened down this drive by accident.

The child in Hope's arms grew fussy. Penny took the baby from her. "He's probably hungry." Penny moved away to feed the infant.

Hope went with Hunter to the covered front windows. "What do you think they are doing out there?"

Hunter held her gaze. "I wish I knew." The tenderness on her pretty face was bittersweet. He cared for her so much. He wanted to believe she had feelings for him, as well. But what *gut* would it do them now when there was a chance no one in this house would make it out alive?

He cupped her face in his hands and just looked deep into her eyes for the longest time. He hated to let her go, but they must finish this once and for all.

"Go back to the others. I'll only be a second."

She reluctantly left him.

His hand shook as he lifted the edge of the curtain just enough to see outside. Nothing but darkness beyond the chilled window. Had the SUV seen the state of the house and figured no one lived there?

A sigh slipped from his body. "I don't see

anything," he said. They'd wait for a little while and then head to the vehicle. Reaching Mason was imperative. He tried to imagine Mason's reaction to hearing what they'd gone through and almost smiled.

The curtain fell from his fingers. He turned to where Hope stood at the edge of the hall watching him with fearful eyes.

He started her way. Hope's face relaxed into a smile, the promise it represented making everything they'd gone through worth it. He'd almost reached her side when the noise of glass breaking stopped him in his tracks. A half second later, he realized what had happened. A bullet had lodged in the wall near where Hope stood. In an instant, the smile disappeared from her face.

"Get down!" he yelled and turned toward the window. More glass shattered. The world around him exploded. He'd been wrong. Those men knew exactly where to find Penny and they were moving in for the kill.

THIRTEEN

Hope hit the floor as the living room filled with gunfire. She couldn't take her eyes off Hunter. He crawled toward her, and she stretched out her hand to reach him. She had to reach him.

"Hurry, Hunter." The words came out as a sob. His fingers touched hers. He covered the gap between them and gathered her close, scrambling behind the wall separating the hallway from the living room.

Hope couldn't stop shaking over what they'd gone through. She noticed Hunter holding the same arm that had gotten grazed by a bullet before. "Are you hurt?"

He moved his hand. It was covered in blood.

"Were you shot again?" Hope helped him remove his coat.

"I don't think so," he murmured.

Through the darkness, Hope did her best to examine the wound. A piece of glass had embedded itself in Hunter's arm. She carefully dislodged the object. Taking off her soaked prayer *kapp*, she used it to wrap around the gash to stop the bleeding.

"We don't know how many are out there," Hunter told the frightened group. "If we try to slip out the back, I'm afraid they will have people waiting there."

Hope turned to Penny. "Is there another way out?"

Penny hesitated only a second. "The basement has a walk-out door, but it's been nailed shut for years. Even if we can get it open, they could be waiting for us."

Yet if they stayed here without trying everything possible, it would end in their deaths.

"What direction does the basement open?"

She glanced down at her son. "At the side of the house. There are woods all around, though. They could be anywhere."

"We have to try," Hope told Hunter. She didn't want to die here. Didn't want to lose him again.

"Come with me to check the basement. Everyone else, wait here."

Beyond the front walls, the shooting had stopped. "I wonder what they are waiting for." She stood next to Hunter at the end of the hall. The open space between their current location and the kitchen with the basement entrance lay in front of them. They'd be exposed until they reached the kitchen.

If she was going to die today, she was glad it would be with the people she cared about the most. And the man who still held her heart.

Hope tucked her hand in Hunter's, pulled in a breath and stepped into the open. The expected attack didn't happen, yet it wasn't a comfort. Jackson and his goons were out there somewhere.

When they reached the kitchen, they turned to a door off to the left that would lead to the basement.

Hope twisted the doorknob. It opened freely in her hand. She pulled in a staccato breath and started inside, but Hunter stopped her.

"Let me go in first. Stay close behind me. We can't use the lights." He stepped onto the basement landing. Nothing but pitch black.

Hope placed her left hand on Hunter's shoulder and the other on the banister.

Each step felt as if she were walking off that cliff again. Several times, Hope stepped on Hunter's foot before they finally reached the bottom stair.

Straight ahead were a couple of windows covered with curtains.

"Where's the door?" Hope whispered.

"Penny said to the side of the house." Hunter

kept her hand in his and started for one of the walls. "Here," he said when his hand connected to the door.

"How do we get the nails free?" As much as she would stand beside Hunter and protect him no matter what, her worst fear was that they'd step through the door and into an ambush.

Hunter took out his pocketknife. He found the first nail in the doorframe and worked it free. Eventually he'd reached the final one.

"Why don't you stay here? Let me check outside first."

She loved him for trying to protect her, but she wouldn't take the coward's way out. "We go together."

Hunter carefully released the lock as quietly as possible before he opened the door and stepped out into the blizzard once more. They faced an L-shaped exterior wall. The roof extended over a walkway to provide protection from rain, or in this case, the snow and sleet.

Hope stayed close to Hunter as they eased along the long wall to the corner of the house.

He looked around the corner. "I don't see anything." He pointed back to the house. Hope turned and headed for the walk-out door. Once they were inside, he relocked it. "Let's get everyone down here as fast as possible. If we can make it to the woods, we might be able to slip around to the front without them seeing. Maybe we can reach their vehicle. Use it to get away."

Navigating the stairs proved every bit as hard as before. Hope clutched his arm until they reached the landing.

As soon as they stepped into the kitchen, another round of gunshots resounded through the house. Hunter grabbed her and ducked behind the wall. When the house grew quiet again, he waved everyone over. "We might be able to make it out through the basement if we hurry."

With Naomi held close, Conrad ran for the protection of the kitchen. *Daed* carried the baby while he and Penny crossed the danger zone.

"It is dark down there," Hunter warned. "Hold on to the banister and be careful." Hope looked at Naomi as he said it. The thought of her taking a fall after everything she'd gone through was unimaginable.

Hope followed Hunter like before. Naomi held on to her shoulder while they descended the steps one by one.

"The door is over here." Hunter headed to the opening. "We must be as quiet as possible to not call attention to ourselves. Conrad, can you and Abe fall to the back? We can use your shooting skills just in case."

Neither man hesitated.

Hunter carefully opened the door and stepped out into the relentless weather.

At the edge of the house, Hunter leaned forward enough to look before facing Hope. "I don't see anything." The uncertainty in his eyes worried her. "Let me see if I can make it to the woods before you bring the others."

He stepped from the protection. Hope held her breath. Nothing but the noise of the storm. Another step, followed by another. The tension wound between her shoulders relaxed slightly. It was going to be *oke*.

"Get ready to follow Hunter," she told the rest. Snow clung to her eyelashes as she willed Hunter to reach the protection without incident. Only a couple of steps separated him from the first group of trees. And then her worst nightmare turned to reality. The woods around them lit up with gunfire.

"Hunter!" Hope screamed above the noise and watched in horror as he ducked low and ran for her.

Hope leaned past the side of the house and began shooting. She'd do whatever she could to keep him safe.

"Get everyone inside," she told Conrad without budging. Bullets landed all around Hunter.

"Go, Hope," he urged when he was still some distance away. "I'll be right behind you."

She wouldn't leave him. The terror on his face scared her. She continued to shoot in the direction of the gunmen until he'd reached cover.

Hope grabbed his hand and pulled him along behind her to where Conrad stood framed in the open walk-out door.

Bullets came from all directions as the shooters advanced on them. The door felt impossible to reach.

Both Conrad and her father stepped outside and opened fire. Hope flew past them with Hunter and pulled him inside. The two men quickly followed and slammed the door shut behind them. Conrad engaged the lock and then gathered his wife close. "That won't give them much of a challenge." He indicated the lock.

Hunter heaved out several labored breaths before answering. "Let's find something to secure the door and then we'll get everyone upstairs and out of danger."

She and Hunter searched for something big enough to block the door.

"There. That old pool table."

It took all the men to get it against the door.

"Should we try the sheriff again?" Hope wondered aloud. At this point, the men knew where they were hiding, and it might be their only hope to survive.

Hunter brought out one of the phones and powered it up.

"There's no answer still," Hunter told her when the call didn't go through. He ran his hand across his eyes. "I remember seeing my *bruder*'s satellite phone number once. It was taped to the back of the phone. If I could remember it, we might be able to reach Mason. I'm thinking it's only the landlines that are down."

Hunter stared at the numbers on the phone before trying several different combinations without any results. His frustration grew. "I can't remember."

Hope clutched his arm. "It will come to you."

Hunter composed himself and dialed another time. He grabbed her arm. "It's him. Mason!" he shouted with relief. "Can you hear me? Mason." He lowered the phone. "It was him, but the call dropped."

Hunter tried again. "Mason. Mason, are you there? I need your help." Another dropped call seemed to mock them with how close they were to being saved.

"He can't hear me. There is too much static on the line." Hunter dialed again. "It's going through. Mason, we are under attack and I am down the road from you. At the first *Englischer* home up the mountain from yours, the one that's been vacant—" He cringed and closed his eyes before ending the call. "I don't know if he heard me."

After several more failed attempts, he gave up. "The service is too bad. I sure hope he heard the location."

"We should get everyone upstairs," Hope said and tried not to give up.

"I believe he heard enough of the conversation to find us. We just have to hold on."

He was trying to remain positive. She would, too.

Something slammed against the door. The men were attempting to gain entrance.

"Hurry, everyone. Upstairs." Hope followed Hunter up the stairs as fast as they dared. Inside the kitchen, Hunter moved one of the heavy wooden chairs against the basement entrance and braced it.

At least that would make it a challenge for them. Down below, the battering continued.

"Let's barricade the front and rear doors, as well."

"I've got the back." Conrad carried another chair over to the rear entrance and placed it below the handle.

Hunter tried the phone again while Hope kept her attention on his face. He shook his head. "Nothing."

"But you reached him. He knows you're in

trouble and he has an idea of the general location. He will come for us." Hope did her best to keep up a positive front, but her faith was fading fast. When she'd woken the day before, nothing in her life had given any indication what lay ahead for her and those who were involved.

"How long before they force their way inside?" she whispered low enough for only Hunter to hear.

"Not long. Whether or not they know Penny is here no longer matters. They found us and they can't let us live, so they will do whatever it takes to prevent us from identifying them."

Hope tried not to fall apart. The thought of having to face these men again was terrifying and she knew Hunter saw it on her face.

He gathered her close. "Hey, don't give up, Hope. We aren't finished yet. We have to keep fighting. No matter what, we have to do whatever we can to stop them." He looked over to where Penny stood with her child. "They have taken enough from her and others. They have to be stopped."

She placed her arms around his waist and held him close. More than ever, she needed his strength. If they survived, it didn't matter what their future held—whether there was a chance for them again or if it was too late—being with Hunter reminded her of the way she'd imagined her future. Just for a brief moment, she got to live what their future should have been. She thought about the things they discussed. The beautiful *haus* he'd built. The *kinner Gott* would bless them with. The love they'd share.

She smiled against his chest and remembered all the times she'd visited Hunter when he and his *bruders* worked on the house. Every decision had been carefully gone over. Hunter used to tease her by saying he wanted ten little ones. And she'd laugh and swat his arm and tell him that was too much. Now it sounded almost perfect.

If she could turn back time and change the outcome of that day, she'd never let him go again.

Hunter held her close and continued to try to reach his *bruder*. Each attempt resulted in the same outcome.

He shoved the phone back into his pocket and prayed Mason would find them. Over Hope's head, his troubled gaze went to the back door. Anyone standing out there could see them through the window in it. With the storm and the darkness, the people inside the house would never know what was coming until the attack hit.

"Let's move one of the chairs against the front doorknob."

"I've got it," Conrad said and carried the chair over. He wedged it beneath the handle. "We need to get everyone back to the hall and out of sight." Hunter let Hope go.

She gathered her father and Penny while he waited beside Conrad and Naomi. "You go first," Hunter told her. "We'll follow."

Hope kept her attention on him for a moment longer before agreeing.

"You get on the other side of me, *dochder*," Abe said, "We'll keep Penny and the *boppli* between us."

"Go quickly," Hunter told Abe. The old man nodded. Once they reached safety, something caught his attention near the back door. Someone was out there.

"Go, Conrad. Take Naomi and hurry." He gave the two a push toward the hall. Hunter aimed at the shadowy figure and fired. A man cried out. Hunter shot again, then ran for cover.

Two steps. Almost there.

"Hurry, Hunter." Inches separated them when the whole outdoors lit up with gun barrel flashes at the front and back of the house. Hunter dived for cover. He hit the floor hard and slammed his injured arm against it. He crawled toward Hope. She grabbed hold of his arms and dragged him the rest of the way out of danger as bullets tore through the house, shattering everything in their range.

Hunter scrambled to his feet and tugged Hope away from the ambush while adrenaline poured through his body. He had to believe Mason was on the way. It was what kept him going. His *bruder* would do everything in his power to find them. With his sat phone, Mason could reach the sheriff and bring them help. Hunter had to do his part and keep them alive until that happened.

"We have to keep fighting," he told the woman who possessed his heart. "Get everyone into another room and out of sight."

She shook her head. "I'm not leaving you."

Someone tried to enter through the back door.

"Hurry, Hope." He gently pushed her toward one of the closed doors before easing down the hall and firing at the person trying to enter the house.

Hunter glanced behind him and saw Hope moving everyone into the last room at the end of the hall.

He shot again and then spun toward the front of the house where another man was trying to shove the door open.

Someone touched his arm. Acting on instinct alone, he jerked toward the touch and saw Hope standing there. She handed him her weapon.

He searched her face. He loved her so much. "Hope…" Before he could bare his heart, the shooting started again and he ducked low. With his arm around her shoulders, he kept her close as the truth became clear.

"It's only a matter of time before they storm the house," he said against her ear so she could hear over the noise. "They are coming in one way or another. We just have to stay alive until Mason gets here."

Tears shimmered in her eyes.

"Stay alive, Hope. For me." The noise of shooting raged around them. The front door splintered, followed by the back. "Hurry." He started toward the back of the house where the others were hiding.

They raced through the door and slammed it closed. Some sort of extra living space spread out before them.

"Help me find something to put in front of the door." With Conrad and Abe's help, he moved a large filing cabinet into place. It would only buy them limited time.

He looked around and realized there was another room off the study. A closet.

"Penny, take the baby and get into the closet. Naomi, you go, as well." He sought out Hope.

She shook her head. "I'm staying. This is my fight, too."

Hunter slowly nodded. Voices could be heard inside the house. They'd search the whole place. It was only a matter of time before they narrowed their hiding spot down to here.

Gott, we need Your help. We cannot fight them on our own. Give us Your strength. Protect us.

The prayer churned up from deep in his heart. He put his arm around Hope, and it felt as natural as taking his next breath.

Feeling her trembling, he wished he could make it better for her—for everyone—but it was an impossible wish.

"Search the place." Hunter recognized that voice from earlier up on the road. He'd been the one talking about having someone else to lead them to Penny. "You—come with me. They can't be far."

Multiple footsteps started down the hall to where he and Hope had been minutes earlier.

"Behind the desk." Hunter pointed to an enormous wooden desk at the back of the room. There was just enough space for everyone to get out of sight.

One by one, the rooms were searched. Footsteps clambered closer. The cabinet wouldn't put up much resistance against so many.

"There's no one here," another familiar voice

could be heard saying. "They can't have gotten away."

"They're here." This was the man from the road. "Try this door."

Footsteps halted outside the study.

Hunter held Hope closer while his heart beat so loud he couldn't hear much else.

The doorknob rattled. Someone shoved hard against it.

"Something's blocking the door," a different man said.

"Get it open." The man in charge growled out the words. "They are in there. We've wasted enough time with them. The cops could be on their way by now."

Hunter rose up enough to see above the desk. The cabinet moved forward. The shoving continued. Another push and it would be free.

Come on, Mason. Hunter thought about trying to fight them to allow the others a chance to escape, but it would end in his death and probably theirs. They'd be picked off until these men would eventually find the one person they were after. Everyone else was just in the way.

FOURTEEN

Hunter lowered himself beside her. "They're coming in now. They'll find us here eventually. Don't do anything to make yourself a target," he warned.

A final shove sent the cabinet tumbling onto its side. The door slammed against the wall. This was it. This was Hope's worst nightmare.

"Find them!" the leader yelled the command to his people. This had to be Stephen Jackson.

Multiple footsteps entered the room.

"Check behind that desk," the same man said.

Hope held on to Hunter tight. Would they kill them right away or force them to give up Penny?

Several people came their way. A breath later, four armed men drew down on them.

"We've got them," one of the men said and tossed a nasty smile over his shoulder. "On your feet. Now." The last word was filled with so much anger, it made Hope jump.

The man grabbed her arm and pulled her away from Hunter. He tried to follow her, but another man stepped between them. He forced the gun from Hunter's hand.

Conrad and her *daed* were yanked to their feet.

"You're hurting him," Hope cried out when the man near her father grabbed hold of his arm and twisted it behind his back.

"Be quiet," her captor spewed. He held her arm so tight, it hurt. They were all forced over to another man standing near the door.

Hope didn't recognize him, but he clearly knew her. He slowly closed the space between them. "You've caused a lot of trouble. You and your Amish people." His irritated glare encompassed the ones standing near her. "You got our people killed." He swung to one of his men. "Check the closet. They can't be far."

The man moved to the closet and opened the door. Hope held her breath while he stuck his head inside. The space was deep, and Penny and Naomi had gotten as far away from the door as possible, hiding behind some hanging coats.

"There's no one here." The man returned shaking his head.

Hope breathed out a sigh. Naomi, Penny and the child were safe for now. If she could keep the men distracted until Mason arrived…

Just when she didn't think the man in charge could come any closer, he did. With a breath separating their faces, the evil she saw in his eyes had her recoiling.

"Where is she." His voice was just above a whisper, yet there was no mistaking it wasn't a question but a demand.

Hope was shaking all over. She did her best to keep from showing it.

"We don't know what you're talking about." Hunter. He was attempting to protect her still. She tried to turn her head. If she could just see him, she wouldn't feel so frightened. The man holding her arm blocked her path.

"Keep him quiet," the leader demanded. A scuffle sounded. What was happening? Hunter screamed. No! Her heart plummeted. She was terrified of what they had done to him and worried for everyone she cared about.

"Stop. Please, don't hurt him." Her voice broke.

The man standing before her smiled. "You care about him? Then you'd better talk. Where is Penny? I know she's hiding." He looked around the room in disgust. "This is her family home."

His dark eyes bored into hers. "Where is she?"

Hope wouldn't give up the young mother.

The man glared, then hauled back and slapped her hard. Her head spun sideways and her eyes teared up.

"Oh, no, you don't," someone behind her said. Another pain-racked scream from Hunter. Hope couldn't think about what they were doing to him and resist trying to reach him.

"She's not here." Hope squared her shoulders while her mind raced over an explanation he would buy. "But I know where she is."

He clearly had doubts. "You're lying. You're trying to protect her." He looked around the room. His eyes glancing past the door to the deep closet where Penny and Naomi hid.

"It's the truth. She's at the house down from here."

His narrowed eyes returned to her. "Really? And why would she be there?"

"Because the person who owns the place is a friend." Hope had no way of knowing if Penny had ever met Mason and his *fraa*. She would have said anything to put a kernel of doubt into his head.

"Really?" He looked from Hope to the rest of the people held captive. "Are you willing to stake his life on that?" He nodded to someone. Her father was brought forward.

Daed's troubled gaze shot to Hope.

"He doesn't know anything. Let him go."

"He's not going anywhere. If you're telling the truth, you have nothing to worry about." He stepped away from Hope and in front of her father. Hope held *Daed*'s gaze.

"I love you, *Daed*," she whispered.

His eyes teared. "I love you, too, *dochder*."

She was in an impossible situation. If she kept silent, this awful man would hurt her father. If she gave Penny's hiding place away, then they all would end up dead once these men got what they wanted from Penny.

The one in charge slammed his fist against her father's midsection.

"No!" she yelled and watched as her *daed* doubled over in pain, the breath sucked from his body in a groan.

She couldn't stand by and let him hurt the man who had been there for her all her life. "I'm telling you the truth. If you come with me, I'll show you."

The leader swung toward her. "So you can lead us away from Penny. Protect these people? I don't think so." He faced her *daed* again and pulled the gun from his waistband. "Last chance. If you want to save your father, you'd better tell me where Penny is hiding."

Her father shook his head to warn her not to say a word. How could she let him die? But how could she bring harm to Penny?

The gun was inches from her father's temple. "What's it going to be? You have to the count of three." He leveled a hard look her way. "One. Two."

"Stop!" Penny stepped from the closet into the room alone. "Don't hurt him, Stephen. I'm right here."

Hunter stared at the nightmare unfolding around him. One of the men moved over to Penny and jerked her toward Jackson.

"Where's the baby?" Jackson looked her up and down. "You've obviously given birth."

Penny didn't respond.

Jackson motioned to one of his men. "Check that closet again. Bring me the child."

The man slipped into the space and came back with a gun pointed at Naomi, who held the *boppli*.

Penny reached for her child, but Jackson took the baby from Naomi before Penny could grasp her son.

"He looks like a little Frank," he said with a nasty grin on his face.

"Give him to me," Penny pleaded. "Please, Stephen."

Jackson ignored her. "I have something you want. You have something I want. Where's the money, Penny? I know you have it."

Penny's attention stayed on her son. "I don't have the money. Frank turned it in."

Stephen glared at her. "That's a lie. It's here somewhere. Don't make me have to search the entire house. Tell me where it is, and you and the rest of these people can go about your day."

Hunter had no doubt he was lying. They'd kill them all. *Please hurry, Mason.*

"I'm not lying. I don't have the money." Penny lifted her chin and stuck to her story.

The anger on Jackson's face turned it bright red. "Bring him to me," he said without looking away from Penny.

The man standing close hurried from the room.

"You know, it was awfully nice of your grandmother to give you this place," Jackson continued. There was something coming. Something bad. "It would be a shame if she should turn up dead."

Terror filled every inch of Penny's face. "My grandmother doesn't live here anymore," she whispered.

"No, she doesn't. She lives in Eagle's Nest. Imagine my surprise when I realized it wasn't all that far from you and Frank."

"What did you do?" Penny lunged for Jackson. Another man grabbed her arms, keeping her in place.

Two sets of footsteps approached from the hall. One sounded as if they were being forced.

The man who'd left entered the room, pulling a second in behind him.

"Frank!" Penny fought to free herself from her restrainer. "You're alive." She sobbed with joy.

Penny's husband had been beaten severely, his face bloody and bruised. He held his side as if it hurt.

"I'm sorry, babe. I tried to keep them from figuring it out."

Stephen faced Penny again. "That's actually true. He held out for a long time. Until we brought the old lady over. I guess the thought of watching her die because he kept his mouth shut was too much for old Frank here. He offered to help us find the house and so I sent for him. Frank almost didn't make it because of this storm. Thankfully, they managed to get through before that tree blocked the road."

Jackson pitched a smug smile at his cousin. "My buddy's watching the old lady. So, you see, if you don't tell me where the money is, I'll have her killed."

"No, please, you can't hurt her, she's not well." Penny begged the man who had no conscience. "Please, this doesn't involve her."

"It didn't until you made it involve her. You

and your husband tried to pull a fast one and take the money for yourselves."

"That's not what happened. We never wanted any part of what's happening, Stephen," Frank told his cousin. "You brought this to us. I just want to live my life with my wife and child." He looked at the baby in Jackson's arms. "I have a son. Please just leave us alone. We won't tell anyone."

Jackson hesitated. Was it possible there was an ounce of decency in this man? Hunter prayed he would let them live.

"Then all you have to do is tell me where the money is, and we'll be gone." Jackson faced Penny again. "Give me the money. You can have your baby and your husband."

"And my grandmother? You won't hurt her?" Penny was obviously desperate to believe Jackson would do the right thing.

He nodded. "Of course. The old lady will be fine."

Penny glanced at her husband, who slowly nodded.

"All right. It's in the basement. I hid it behind the bookcase."

Jackson shoved the baby at Frank. "Jim, go with her. Don't let her try anything. Bring me the money."

The man called Jim grabbed Penny and forced

her from the room. Hunter's mind raced to figure out a way to save their lives. He had no way of knowing for certain Mason had heard enough of the conversation to know where they were. Once Jackson had the money, Hunter was convinced they'd kill every single one of them.

He glanced around the room for something to assist. A fireplace with a set of tools was against the far wall. If he could create a distraction, it might be possible to reach the tools to use as a weapon. Against so many armed men, he'd be killed before he ever got close. The only other option was to overpower the men.

He got Conrad's attention. *We have to take them down.* He mouthed the words.

Conrad nodded.

"Hey, what are you trying to do?" the man holding Hunter demanded. "Stop talking to him." He jerked Hunter's arm hard.

"Conrad." Hunter ignored the man. Conrad nodded. His friend would do whatever he said. Would it cost Conrad his life?

Jackson strode toward Hunter. "Are you going to try to be a hero? That's a good way to end up dead."

Hunter managed to hold back his fear. "I'm not trying to be anything. I care about these people and I want to keep them safe."

Jackson's eyes narrowed. "You heard me say we'd be gone once we have the money."

Hunter looked into the man's eyes and knew he was lying. "I also know you're not telling the truth."

Jackson slowly smiled and leaned closer so only Hunter heard him say, "You're right. I'm not." As the terrible reality penetrated Hunter's tangled thoughts, Jackson slammed the handgun against Hunter's head. The world and his fear shut down.

FIFTEEN

"Hunter!" Hope shouted and tried to free herself as Hunter dropped unconscious to the floor. "Let me go." She struggled with all her strength, but she was no match for her captor.

Jackson stared down at Hunter's motionless body with a satisfied look on his face. Tears burned the backs of Hope's eyes. Jackson was a liar. She'd seen the truth in his eyes. He wasn't a man of his word. He would kill them.

Jim returned with a duffel bag slung over his shoulder, holding Penny's arm in a vise grip.

Jackson moved to stand in front of Penny. "You brought this on yourself and everyone else." He motioned to the man holding her. "Get them tied up."

Penny sobbed. "Stephen, you promised to let us go."

Jackson ignored her.

Hope's legs grew weak. "You don't have to

do this. Take the money and leave. We won't tell anyone."

"Shut up." Jackson snatched the bag from his man and looked inside. With a satisfied nod, he fixed his attention on Hope. "You think I'd believe a word you say? As soon as we're gone, you're going to contact the sheriff."

"No, we won't," Hope told him. "The Amish don't believe in bringing in law enforcement to settle disputes. We are pacifists." She kept talking—trying to convince this heartless man to let them live. "You can leave. You don't have to worry about us turning you in."

Jackson's eyes burned into her before he laughed. "You almost had me, Amish girl." He strode to the door. "Tie them up. Starting with her." He pointed straight at Hope.

Hope's legs deserted her. The man confining her held her up while another man secured her hands in front of her, followed by her ankles. Once he'd finished, he shoved her to the ground and moved to her *daed*.

Her eyes grabbed onto *Daed*'s and held while his hands were forced in front of him. They shoved her father to the floor beside Hope.

"It will be *oke*," she whispered, though she didn't believe it. These men wouldn't be tying them up if they intended to let them live.

"My baby!" Penny screamed when the child

was taken from Frank's arms by one of the men. Once Frank was secured, the *boppli* was placed on the floor in front of him. The child, most likely sensing danger, began to cry.

Tears streamed down Penny's face while they tied her up and placed her beside Frank. With her hands restrained, she couldn't hold her child. Hope couldn't imagine anything more heart-breaking for the young mother.

Penny leaned over the child and did her best to soothe her son.

Watching Naomi being handled so roughly was hard to take. Hope wanted to scream for them to leave her friend alone. At least the man who restrained her had the decency to assist her to the floor.

If they survived this nightmare, would the stress of what she'd suffered be too much? Conrad had confided once he didn't believe his *fraa* would survive another miscarriage. She couldn't lose this one.

Please, Gott, *help us. Please bring Mason soon.*

Naomi's frightened face turned to Hope. Though her heart raced, and her frightened breaths came quickly, Hope did her best to comfort her friend.

Once Conrad was placed beside Naomi, several men went over to where Hunter remained unconscious. He still wasn't moving. Hope's heart clenched.

Jackson ordered his men to get him on his back. Hunter groaned at the shift. He was alive.

"Denki. Oh, *denki,"* Hope sobbed. If they were going to die like this, she wanted to tell him how much she still loved him. Wanted him to know she was sorry for hurting him.

One man leaned over and tied the rope tight around Hunter's wrists. Hunter winced and opened his eyes.

The man smiled when he realized Hunter was awake. "Welcome to the party."

Hunter kicked out, taking the man by surprise. He stumbled backward, a stream of curse words flying from his lips. Once he'd righted himself, he stormed back to Hunter and slapped him hard. "Try that again and you'll be dead before the others."

Hunter's head flew sideways. Two additional men converged to hold Hunter's legs while the first man secured them.

"Get him up and over to the rest," he told the others.

Each grabbed Hunter under an arm and hauled him up. They dragged him along the floor and dropped him next to Conrad.

With a final glare Hunter's way, the man and

his friends moved over to where Jackson stood near the door.

"What's the plan, Stephen?" the same man asked while tossing a dark look at them over his shoulder. "We can't just leave them here. They've seen our faces."

Jackson repositioned the money bag. "We'll take care of them, but we've gotta get out of this miserable community afterward and we have to do it quickly."

"What about the tree blocking the road?"

"See if you can find something to get it out of the way." Jackson didn't realize there was another way out of the area on this side of the mountain. "And do it fast." He glanced at the windows before flicking a look at Penny. "Do you have a chain saw or an ax?"

Penny's bottom lip trembled. "I… I don't know." Jackson's face flushed with rage. "Wait, yes, there is a chain saw. In the garage. It belonged to my grandfather."

Jackson swung toward two of his men. "Well, what are you waiting for? Go get it." The two hurried from the room.

Hope leaned forward until she could see Hunter. He turned his head to her. The tenderness on his face had her forcing back another sob. *Too late.* The words kept playing through her head. She still loved him. She'd love him until she drew her last breath here on earth. Would that moment come with a bullet to her head? Or would she and the others find a way out before these men finished what they had planned and killed all witnesses?

Hope's pretty face was marred by a bright red mark across her cheek—evidence of the damage left behind by men's greed. He couldn't let it end like this. Not with a child's life in jeopardy. Not when Naomi had come so close to delivering a healthy *boppli*. Not when he had found Hope again.

"Don't give up," he told her. Her eyes filled with tears before she slowly nodded.

"I won't."

"Keep quiet," Jackson demanded. "Or I'll put a bullet in the both of you."

Jackson scowled at them but didn't say anything more. Still, the threat hung in the air. Hunter flexed his wrist. There was no way he could work the rope free on his own. He watched Jackson and the rest of his people while his mind fought to find a way to save their lives. His pocketknife was in his pocket. If he could reach it…

He moved his bound hands over to the pocket, but he couldn't get into position to reach it with them tied.

Hunter nudged Conrad. *Pocketknife*, he mouthed as to not warn the others. He indicated the pocket.

Conrad slowly nodded and cut his eyes toward the men.

If they spotted any movement, would they search them? Find the knife. He couldn't think about that and not lose hope. Hunter prayed for a distraction.

"We found it." The two returned with a chain saw, and Jackson and the others shifted toward them.

"Now," Hunter whispered and inched as close to Conrad as he possibly could. Conrad somehow managed to get his bound hands inside the pocket.

"And we found this," one man said. He held up two containers. Gas cans. The truth dawned with horrifying clarity. Jackson and his goons were going to set the house on fire with them in it. Wipe away any evidence they may have left behind. Silence any witnesses against them.

"I have the knife," Conrad whispered.

Hunter continued to watch Jackson. His smile sent a tremor through Hunter's frame. It had nothing to do with humor.

"That should do it." Jackson stepped over to his cousin. "I am sorry it had to end like this, Frank. All you had to do was keep your mouth shut and stay put. Not try to keep the money for yourself."

Frank's broken body reflected the extent of the pain he'd experienced at his cousin's hands. "I want nothing to do with that money. I was going to have Penny leave it somewhere and I'd tell you where to find it. I just wanted to save Penny's and my child's lives."

Jackson's expression hardened. He leaned down into his cousin's face. "You think I believe that. You planned to turn us in before we even got out of the county. You betrayed blood. Now you all will pay for it. Oh, and Frank, the old lady is going to die, too."

Frank lunged for him. Jackson stepped back and Frank fell forward. "Leave her alone. She doesn't know anything about the bank robbery."

"That doesn't really matter to me. This money should be enough for us to start over in South America, in a country that doesn't have an extradition treaty with the US." He nodded to the person with the gas containers. The man handed one to his partner and they began splashing the fuel around the room.

"Don't forget the rest of the house. I want nothing but embers left by the time the fire department gets here." Jackson never looked away from his cousin. "I'd like to say I'll see you again Frank, but we both know that isn't going to happen." With an ugly grin, he turned on his heel and headed for the door.

As his men filed from the room, Jackson took something from his pocket. Matches. Hunter's heart dropped. Once the match hit the gas, the room would go up like a tinderbox. Even if he could free his hands with the knife, would there be enough time to save every person in the room?

Jackson took great pleasure in slowly striking the match to the flint on the pack. It caught right away. He held it up, enjoying tormenting them. Then he slowly tossed it to the soaked floor. The gas caught in a whoosh, and Jackson laughed as he left the room.

The gas trail became a path for the fire. As soon as it reached the curtains, it climbed quickly, disintegrating everything in its path.

Conrad pulled the knife out. It hit the side of Hunter's pocket and dropped to the floor, sliding away from both. Hunter scrambled after it as it landed inches from the flames. Retrieving the blade was their only hope, and it was quickly fading. He grabbed the knife in his hands and carefully brought it up to his lips. Using his teeth, he clamped down on the bit of blade visible until he was able to use the grooved section to open the pocketknife.

Working with hands that shook so much it

was hard to hold the knife, Hunter freed his feet but couldn't get the knife in position to loosen his hands.

Hunter scooted in front of Conrad and transferred the knife to him. Conrad worked steadily to get Hunter's hands unbound.

With them free, Hunter grabbed the knife and started with Conrad's hands while he glanced around the room quickly filling with smoke and fire. Both Conrad and Abe carried knives. If he could get them free, it would make the task of freeing the others faster.

Headlights flashed across the room. Jackson and his people were leaving. Had they left someone behind to make sure everyone inside the house died? He couldn't think about that.

Hunter finally sawed through the final strands of rope, and Conrad was loose. "Get your knife. I'll loosen Abe's hands."

Conrad retrieved his pocketknife.

"Help Naomi and Penny. Get the baby out of here. Go out the back door in case there are some still close."

Hunter hurried to Abe and went to work.

"You should help the others first," Abe told him. "I'm an old man. I've lived my life."

Hunter shook his head. "We need you. Use your knife once you're free. With three of us working together, it will go faster."

The fire quickly spread around the room, igniting furniture that had been sitting uncared for through the years.

Abe's last rope snapped.

"I'll get Hope," Hunter told him.

The older man nodded and moved to Penny's side, pulling out his knife while Conrad helped Naomi and the baby from the house. Hunter was terrified the fire would envelope the house before he could save Hope. He couldn't let that happen.

Conrad returned. "The house is almost completely engulfed in fire. I had to beat off flames to reach the back door. Hurry, Hunter."

It was worse than Hunter thought. "Help the others. Hope and I will be right behind you."

Conrad nodded and assisted Frank while Abe got Penny into the hall.

The smoke swirled around them thick and acrid. He lost sight of Hope.

"Where are you?" he called out in panic. He couldn't see his hands in front of him.

A bout of coughing led him to her.

"I've got you." He knelt at her side and went to work on freeing her from the restraints. Pieces of the ceiling began to fall free. He remembered the heavy pine beams in the middle of the ceiling. If they fell…

His desperate fingers continued to saw. "Hold

on, Hope. I'm almost through." His bleary eyes met hers briefly before he kept working. The rope released. "Use your coat and cover your nose and mouth."

He helped her to her feet while the fire crackled and popped like a beast spreading its wings. The walls were now completely consumed, along with most of the furniture.

Hope pulled her coat up over her nose and mouth while he did the same. Looping his arm through hers, he started in the direction he believed the door to be.

A loud creak had him glancing up. Those overhead beams worried him. How long before they collapsed? If they were hit by one, it would be a fatal blow.

"We're going to have to get down low to conserve oxygen." Both dropped to their knees and crawled. Through the thick grayness, the opening became visible. "Go, Hope. I'm right behind you." She scrambled for the entrance.

A terrifying sound above warned him it was too late. Hunter dived for the door. A blazing beam hurled itself to the floor, barely missing him. The chandelier crashed on top of him while the beam struck the sofa and sent it flying through the air. The piece of furniture landed on his leg. Hunter blacked out for a moment. When he came to, the chandelier was on his chest and he couldn't get himself free. He was trapped.

"Help!" he called out and started coughing.

Hope's beautiful face materialized above him. "I've got you." She grabbed hold of his legs and tried to pull him out from under the debris.

"I have to get this stuff off my leg, otherwise I'm not going anywhere." He lifted himself up on his elbows.

Flames licked all around the room. The smoke stung his eyes and burned his lungs. "Here." Hope slipped past him and tugged the light fixture off. He forced himself to a sitting position and pushed as hard as he could. The sofa didn't budge.

"Hang on, I can move it." Hope reached the side of the sofa and put her arms around it. Against all odds, the sofa moved enough to get his leg free. "Can you get out?" She came back to him and felt around his limbs.

"I can walk," he told her and stumbled to his feet. Pain shot down the leg that took the brunt of the sofa. His chest ached from the chandelier. Hunter winced and tried to put pressure on his leg but couldn't.

"Let me help you." Hope wrapped her arm around his waist. The strength in her was not a surprise. Hope was a strong woman in all ways. She helped him across the burning threshold and into the hall. Everything was on fire. Heat from the fire scorched their faces. Tears streamed from his eyes. Almost to the kitchen.

Hunter wiped his eyes and ignored the pain while Hope guided him. Conrad met them at the back door. With his and Hope's help, they got Hunter outside.

"The others are in the trees." Conrad headed them toward the woods where everyone had gathered some distance away from the smoldering house.

With Hope holding him close, Hunter watched the house blaze. There would be no bringing it back, but everyone had gotten out safely.

"What if they come back to make sure we're dead?" Conrad said.

Hunter stared at the weary faces of the people who had just survived the horrendous attack meant to end their lives. Even standing some distance away, the heat from the fire was intense.

"Let me bring the vehicle around and we'll get everyone inside. Jackson and his people obviously don't know there's another way out that doesn't involve going back over the mountain. That will keep them occupied for a while. It should be safe for us to use the road again."

He glanced down at his leg. It was the one

he'd used to work the gas and brake pedals on the vehicle. He'd have to drive with his left one.

"I am coming with you," Hope told him. She must have seen his concern. "I can drive." Though she'd been hesitant behind the wheel before, Hope had his back.

He smiled his relief. *"Denki."*

Hunter put his arm around her shoulders, while all he could think about was what would happen if Jackson and his goons returned. The heat from the fire made it impossible to get too close to the burning house.

"Wait," he told her when she would have stepped from their hiding place. "They could still be out there." He edged out enough to try to see. The storm peppered him with snow while the howling wind hit him head-on. There was no way to see anything.

"Let's keep going." They moved toward the garage. If he and Hope could find Mason, it was possible to get the sheriff here before Jackson and his people got away.

Hope turned the doorknob and helped him inside.

"How are you holding up?" she asked with concern for him that took the chill from his heart.

"I'm holding on," he said through gritted teeth.

Hope opened the passenger door and he stumbled onto the seat and shifted his injured leg around in front of him.

She closed the door and got behind the wheel, then started the vehicle and looked down to the floor. "There's no clutch?" Her brows rose as she faced him.

"It's automatic, like the first car. You just put it in Drive and go."

Hunter closed his eyes and fought against nausea.

Hope eased from the garage and started forward. She leaned in close to the windshield. "I can't believe they were willing to kill for money."

He did his best to help her watch for any danger. His body craved rest and to be able to simply relax without fear of dying. Letting down their guard for a second wasn't an option.

"Oh, no," Hope whispered and hit the brake.

Hunter saw the headlights. Jackson and his people must have returned to make sure there were no witnesses.

"Turn around and go back to the garage as fast as you can," he told her while he couldn't take his eyes off the lights moving toward them.

Hope eased the vehicle around on the drive. It spun out several times as she tried to get it moving forward.

"Stop for a second and let off the gas." Hope did as he suggested. "Now, try it again, but only give it a little gas."

She pulled in a breath and pushed down on the pedal. The tires spun once, then lurched forward.

Hope started for the garage while Hunter watched the other vehicle moving faster than he expected.

"Give it more gas. They're coming up quickly." He tried not to give in to the hopelessness. They'd fought so hard to survive everything Jackson had thrown at them, including a fire meant to kill them all. Now, when he wanted this to be over, Jackson had returned.

Hope hit the gas and the vehicle glided along the path. She struggled to keep it from sliding into one of the trees along the way.

The house was now fully engulfed, illuminating everything nearby. They had to put the vehicle out of sight and find the others. Get to a safer location.

Hope reached the garage and drove inside. Injured or not, he had to pull his weight.

He struggled to get out. Favoring his injured leg, he shut the overhead door and then reached Hope. "We have to warn everyone."

She slipped her arm around his waist once

more. Together, they moved through the woods as fast as his leg and the conditions would allow.

"There. I see them." Hope pointed to the battered group of people who had survived so much.

Once they were close, Hunter told them what he feared. "Let's go deeper into the woods."

The fearful expression on his friends' faces was hard to take.

From his vantage spot, Hunter could see the lights weaving through the woods. Would they risk going inside a burning house to confirm the deaths or simply wait until the fire had gone out? Such ruthlessness made him physically sick.

The vehicle reached the final bend in the road and stopped. Behind it—and some distance away—another vehicle. Someone else was coming.

"Where did the second vehicle come from?" Hope asked in astonishment.

Nothing about the second vehicle added up. He had watched the car go over the side of the mountain. There wasn't another one around.

"Let's get closer," he told Hope. With her at his side, he moved through the trees until they were opposite the first vehicle.

Through the snow, it was impossible to see more than the headlights reflecting the storm.

Doors opened. The second vehicle stopped and its driver exited. The person in the first moved into the headlights' glow. The relief Hunter felt when he recognized his brother almost dropped him to the ground.

"It's Mason. We're safe. It's my *bruder*. Mason!" Hunter yelled his brother's name as loud as he could and then started through the trees.

"Mason, we're over here." As soon as he and Hope cleared the trees, Mason heard Hunter's voice and spun with a weapon in his hand and ready for use. Mason recognized Hunter and tucked the weapon away before he ran in their direction.

With a few feet separating them, Mason looked him over and then embraced his brother.

"I've been so worried since your call. What on earth happened here?" he asked once he'd let Hunter go.

"*Bruder*, you're not going to believe it. I'm not sure I even do."

Slowly, the others hiding in the woods realized it was safe and came over. Ethan Connors was the driver of the second vehicle. Ethan's attention went to the fire first and then the people gathered around. "What happened?"

Hunter did his best to explain the nightmare they'd endured. "They are heading out of the community. They have a chain saw with them to move the tree blocking the road."

Ethan nodded. "I'll check on the sheriff's ETA. We were able to reach him on his sat phone earlier." He turned away to place the call while Mason noticed Naomi and Penny with the child.

"Let's get everyone out of this weather."

Ethan finished his call and Mason explained he was taking everyone to his home.

"Good idea. Sheriff's on his way here now. I'll wait for him. The fire department is coming to contain the fire so it doesn't spread."

Mason opened the door of the SUV. Thankfully, the bishop allowed him and Fletcher the freedom to use vehicles when it involved their search and rescue operations.

"*Komm*, get inside where it's warm," Hunter told the weary souls with him. The vehicle was big enough to fit them all.

As soon as everyone was inside, Hunter climbed in beside his *bruder*, and Mason didn't waste time leaving the property.

"I can't believe what's happened," Mason said with a look Hunter's way. "The sheriff will want to speak to each of you." Mason glanced back to where Hope sat beside her *daed*. "Perhaps there is something *gut* to come from this terrible thing, after all. Something *gut* indeed."

SIXTEEN

Though the heat of the fire ate at the cold in her body, Hope couldn't seem to get warm. The chill went much deeper than physical. When she thought about what they'd survived in such a short period of time, it seemed impossible. They all had been forced into a situation that tested the very fiber of their faith.

Someone touched her hand. Hope glanced up and found Hunter standing nearby with a cup held out to her. "My sister-in-law Willa made *kaffe*."

She smiled, accepted the cup and held it in her hands, letting its warmth seep through her fingers.

"The fire is out at Penny's home." Hunter slipped into the seat beside her.

Hope glanced over to where Penny and Frank sat with their baby at the kitchen table, quietly talking. "They've been through so much. They didn't deserve any of this."

Hunter watched her for a long moment. "Neither did you. You probably saved Naomi's and the *boppli*'s lives. If you hadn't acted quickly…"

Hope shook her head. "You saved us, Hunter. You got us through the storm and saved us from those terrible men." She hated thinking Jackson and his men would get away with what they'd done.

"Sheriff Collins is on his way here to get our statements," he said, as if reading her thoughts. "His people arrested Jackson and his men and recovered the money."

Thank You, Gott. The tension strung tight between her shoulders slowly faded. "I'm so happy to hear it. What about Penny's grandmother?"

He smiled and clasped her hand. "Safe. Deputies forced their way into her home and overpowered the man holding her hostage. She's fine."

She breathed out a weary sigh. "So, everything worked out."

He nodded. "They did. Those men will be facing a lot of charges, according to Mason. It will be a long time before they get out of prison."

Hope's attention went to the sofa nearby where Naomi rested. "I'm so worried about her. This has been hard for Naomi and the *boppli*."

He followed her line of sight. "*Jah,* I'm worried, as well. The *gut* news is the storm appears to be letting up at last, and it will be daylight soon. Naomi is resting—the best thing for her now. As soon as the sheriff has our statements, I'll use the SUV Mason picked us up in and drive Naomi and Conrad home."

Her attention returned to his handsome face. "I'll *komm* with you. I think I'll stay with them for a while until I am certain she is *oke*."

He hesitated, as if struggling to find the right words. They'd healed old wounds by surviving Jackson's attack. Where did that leave them now?

"Hope…" He started to say more and suddenly she wasn't sure she was ready to hear what came next.

"Wait." The word slipped out. She freed her hand and jumped to her feet, putting several steps between them. Hunter's devastated gaze held hers. He rose slowly and started toward her. Before he reached her side, headlights flashed across the front of the house. Hunter never looked away. The pain in his expression broke her heart again.

Mason opened the door and two people in uniforms came inside. Hope recognized Sheriff Collins. She'd seen the female deputy before, as well.

Hunter pulled his attention from her and

stepped away. She could breathe again. What had really changed? Though she loved him and believed he cared for her, they were still on opposite sides of a disagreement that would never be settled, and she could not desert her father.

Hope spotted her *daed* standing near the window. She joined him. Soon, she and the others would have to relive the nightmare again. The one *gut* thing was that those responsible for so much ugliness would be made to pay, and she would somehow find a way to forgive them because that was the Plain way. Holding on to anger served no purpose. Against her will, she looked at Hunter. She couldn't imagine what would have happened if he had not been there to get them through the ordeal.

Hope looked out at the new day dawning. The storm had finally blown itself out. The threat it posed was over.

"You still care for him." Her father's voice broke into her troubled thoughts. She turned. He'd seen her looking at Hunter.

Hope did her best to deny it. "*Nay*. What was between us is gone."

He shook his head. "It isn't. I've watched you both tonight. Seen the way you look at each other. And I saw the way he handled things. It took a lot of courage. He reminded me of Levi."

Hope looked at the regret on her father's face. "But it's too late."

He reached for her hand. "*Nay, dochder*, it's not. You're both still alive. Coming close to death made me see how I let my anger and grief over losing your *mamm* get in the way of my friendship with Levi. I should have trusted that he would never do anything to hurt me. Levi tried to tell me he'd seen some *Englischer* men with chain saws near my place, but I wouldn't listen. And because of it, I lost a *gut* friend. Don't let that happen to you." *Daed* smiled wearily. "You still care for him and I believe he does for you, as well. You and Hunter shouldn't have to pay for my mistakes." He shook his head. "I'm a tired old man who has lost so much. Don't let this be you one day. Make things right with Hunter while you have the opportunity."

Hope fought back tears. "What if you're wrong? What if he doesn't feel the same way about me?"

Daed squeezed her hands in his. "You'll never know if you don't try. Try, *dochder*. Try."

The drive back to Naomi and Conrad's home was much different than their frantic flight down the mountain hours earlier.

Hope had insisted on sitting beside Naomi in the back seat. She told herself it was to make sure her friend had a painless trip, but in truth, she wasn't ready to have that discussion with Hunter after talking to her father. Not when she felt this vulnerable.

She replayed her father's words in her head as the new day presented a world covered in snow. The blizzard had left behind downed tree limbs everywhere. They traveled at a much slower pace up the mountain where they'd almost died.

Hope was acutely aware of the occasional curious look from Hunter in the rearview mirror. She'd give anything to know his thoughts. If this was really going to be goodbye, she wasn't sure she could handle living in the same community with him. The thought of watching him find someone else eventually brought tears to her eyes.

Naomi clutched her hand tight. Hope ignored her heartache and cast a worried look her friend's way. "Is it the *boppli*?"

Naomi managed a nod. "*Jah*, I believe it's time."

Conrad turned in his seat. "What's wrong?" His troubled eyes found his *fraa*'s.

Naomi tried to smile, but Hope could see she was fearful.

Though a few days early, the child should be fine. "There's nothing to worry about," she told the troubled couple. To Hunter, she said, "We need to get Naomi to her home and into bed as soon as possible."

After everything Naomi had gone through tonight, and the three previous pregnancies that had ended in miscarriage, Hope was going to do everything in her power to give her friend a happy ending and bring this *boppli* safely into her *mamm*'s and *daed*'s arms to love and cherish.

Hunter did his best to keep his friend calm during the waiting. Nothing could be heard coming from the room. Conrad stopped next to the door countless times, started to go inside, then turned and came back to the living room, where he proceeded to pace the small space.

Though physically exhausted, Hunter had a good feeling. Under Hope's expert care, Naomi and the *boppli* would be fine.

His arm and leg had been attended to by Mason once they reached his *bruder*'s home. Though it still hurt to put much weight on the leg, the injuries he'd sustained there were nothing, and he was just happy they were all alive.

"Why is it taking so long?" Conrad muttered.

Hunter clamped his hand on his friend's shoulder. "*Bopplis* come in their own time. You must be patient." Yet the advice felt lacking. He had little experience with children, except for his nieces and nephews. When he'd realized he was in love with Hope, everything had fallen into place. He could almost picture the future they'd have. The *kinner*. But life had taken them down a different direction and the family he'd believed possible had vanished. But he still loved her. And he believed she loved him, with every fiber inside him. He couldn't wait to speak to her about the future.

After much more pacing on Conrad's part, the piercing wail of new life could be heard inside the room. The *boppli* had arrived.

"She's here." Conrad broke into a smile that seemed to be branded on his face. The child they had waited so long for was here.

He hurried to the door and stood outside in anticipation. Time passing felt like forever. Then, finally, Hope opened the door. She jumped back in surprise when she saw Conrad standing so close. Remnants of the nightmare they'd endured bled into this perfect moment.

"*Komm*, meet your *dochder*," she said with a smile and opened the door wide. Hunter hung back, uncertain of his place here.

Conrad motioned him inside. "Would you like to see the *boppli*?"

He did, but he didn't want to intrude.

Conrad lifted the child into his arms and beamed with pride at his wife. "She's beautiful."

Naomi's eyes filled with tears. "*Jah*, she is."

And she was. Hunter peeked at the baby and gave thanks to *Gott* for granting this moment.

"She's special. She will have you wrapped around her little finger before you know it," Hunter told Conrad.

Conrad laughed with joy while his wife quietly wept at their infant.

Hope caught Hunter's attention and motioned him outside. "We'll give you two some private time with the *boppli.*" Both parents were too wrapped up in their bundle of joy to notice them leaving.

She stepped outside with Hunter and quietly closed the door.

"I'm so happy for them," she whispered with a peek his way.

He was, too, but there were other things on his mind. Future things. But now that it was just Hope and him, did he dare lay his heart bare to her?

She didn't look at him as she moved to the fire and warmed her hands. The gesture wasn't in any way encouraging.

Gott, give me the strength to say the things I need to and let her hear them with an open heart.

He went after her and touched her shoulder.

Hope slowly faced him.

"I'm sorry. I didn't mean to startle you."

She blushed and dropped her gaze. "It's fine. I guess I haven't been able to relax since…"

She didn't finish, but he understood. It would take him a while to believe he was finally safe.

"Hope, I love you," he blurted out and slapped his forehead. This was not the way he'd wanted to tell her.

Her brows knitted together with an uncertain look. "You do?"

His mouth twisted in pain. "*Jah*, I do. Of course I do. I never stopped loving you, and I'm sorry that I didn't stand by you back then. I should have. If you will have me again, I will always have your back."

"You love me?" She appeared to be struggling to believe. Tears filled her eyes and she cried as if her heart was breaking.

"No, Hope, don't cry. What is it?" He had to understand if her tears were *gut* or the cause of his heart breaking.

She smiled through the tears. "I'm not sad— well maybe a little. Hunter, what happened back then is just as much my fault as it is yours. I didn't have your back when I should, either. But I will. I promise I will." Hope touched his cheek. "I love you. Always have, even though I tried to deny it."

He gathered her close and kissed her, and it

didn't matter what happened in the future. She loved him. They would figure the rest out.

"My *daed* told me tonight he regretted the argument between him and your father. He said because of his stubborn pride, he let a few cross words destroy their friendship, and he regretted it." She hugged him close. "My father told me he could see we still loved each other and he wanted us to be together."

Hunter was shocked by Abe's admission. "That is *gut* to hear. I was afraid I would have to fight him for the chance to marry you." He smiled tenderly. Hope had borrowed a prayer *kapp* from Mason's wife and pinned her hair back into place, but some had worked free during the delivery. Hunter tucked it behind her ear.

"My *daed* told me how much he regretted losing Abe as a friend. It was one of his biggest regrets. But we won't be them, Hope. Never again will we let anything come between us."

He held her close and was content to stand with her and wait patiently for all the things they each thought had been lost to them. The future was as wide open as the Montana territory surrounding their community. And he couldn't wait to experience all that it had to give them. With this woman in his arms.

EPILOGUE

Two years later...

Hope was nervous. As a midwife, having someone else help deliver her child would not be easy. It wasn't as if she didn't trust Amelia Lehman, because she did. It was just that Hope wasn't accustomed to being on this side of the care. This was her and Hunter's first *boppli*.

Hope glanced out the window at the snow falling and recalled that day when a nightmare resulted in bringing her back to the man she loved. She would forever be grateful for every frightening moment they'd experienced because it made them both realize life is short and meant to be lived without regrets.

She had been blessed to bring Penny and Frank's second *kinna* into the world and thankful that they hadn't let what happened tear them apart. Though their home here in West Kootenai had been destroyed, they'd rebuilt it for their growing family. They visited Penny's grandmother weekly to check up on her.

Hope stopped by often to visit with her friends Naomi and Conrad. It was hard to believe two years had passed since they'd survived those terrible men and young Rose had come into the world. Though Naomi and Conrad wished for more children, they patiently waited for *Gott*'s blessings.

And now it was her and Hunter's turn.

Down the lane, the buggy appeared, and a relieved breath slipped out. Her *mann* had returned, bringing Amelia with him. Suddenly, the moment became real. She was having a baby. She and Hunter were going to be parents.

Hunter stopped the mare in front of the house he and his *bruders* had built for them, and hopped down, quickly assisting Amelia.

He took the porch steps with that long stride of his and opened the door. Once he saw her standing by the window, a smile spread across his face.

"Are you ready?" he asked and hugged her.

In the safety of his arms, she knew the answer was simple. She was ready. So ready to *willkumm* their child into the world. Ready for the rest of their lives. Together.

* * * * *

Dear Reader,

Sometimes, the plans of our youth do not work out the way we imagined. Life, and the decisions we make along the way, can alter our direction. For the better at times, but not always.

No matter how far off course we drift, God is there with us, even when we cannot feel His presence.

For Hope Christner and Hunter Shetler, it was an argument between their fathers that changed their future direction. But God, in His immeasurable mercy, worked out their circumstances perfectly and brought these two injured hearts back together. And He is constantly there to take our hand and pull us out of our bad decisions. We just have to ask Him.

God's blessing to you all,
Mary Alford

Get 4 FREE REWARDS!

We'll send you 2 FREE Books plus 2 FREE Mystery Gifts.

Love Inspired Suspense books showcase how courage and optimism unite in stories of faith and love in the face of danger.

FREE Value Over $20

HARLEQUIN SELECTS COLLECTION

19 FREE BOOKS IN ALL!

From Robyn Carr to RaeAnne Thayne to Linda Lael Miller and Sherryl Woods we promise (actually, GUARANTEE!) each author in the Harlequin Selects collection has seen their name on the *New York Times* or *USA TODAY* bestseller lists!

Get 4 FREE REWARDS!

We'll send you 2 FREE Books <u>plus</u> 2 FREE Mystery Gifts.

Worldwide Library books feature gripping mysteries from "whodunits" to police procedurals and courtroom dramas.

FREE Value Over **$20**